格雷的老爸

格雷的哥哥
——罗德里克

格雷的"死党"
——罗利

格雷的弟弟
——曼尼

格雷梦想中
的小狗

DIARY
of a Wimpy Kid

小屁孩日记⑦

——从天而降的巨债

[美] 杰夫·金尼　著

陈万如　译

格雷的老妈

格雷

·广州·

广东省出版集团

新世纪出版社

本书简体中文版由美国 Harry N. Abrams 公司通过中国 Creative Excellence Rights Agency 独家授权

版权合同登记号：19-2010-057 号

图书在版编目（CIP）数据

小屁孩日记⑦：从天而降的巨债／［美］杰夫·金尼著；

陈万如译. —2 版. —广州：新世纪出版社，2012.6（2016.1 重印）

ISBN 978-7-5405-4460-7/02

Ⅰ. ①小⋯　Ⅱ. ①杰⋯　②陈⋯　Ⅲ. 漫画-作品集-美国-现代　Ⅳ. J238.2

中国版本图书馆 CIP 数据核字（2010）第 224986 号

出　版　人：孙泽军

选题策划：林　铨　王小斌

责任编辑：王小斌　傅　琨

责任技编：王建慧

小屁孩日记⑦——从天而降的巨债

XIAOPIHAI RIJI⑦——CONGTIANERJIANG DE JUZHAI

［美］杰夫·金尼　著　陈万如　译

出版发行：新世纪出版社

（广州市大沙头四马路 10 号　邮政编码：510102）

经　　销：全国新华书店

印　　刷：广东省教育厅教育印刷厂

开　　本：890mm×1240mm　1/32

印　　张：6.75　字　数：130 千字

版　　次：2011 年 1 月第 1 版　2012 年 6 月第 2 版

印　　次：2016 年 1 月第 22 次印刷

印　　数：222 001～272 000

定　　价：16.80 元

质量监督电话：020-83797655　购书咨询电话：020-83781545

"小屁孩之父" 杰夫·金尼致中国粉丝

中国的"哈屁族"：

你们好!

从小我就对中国很着迷,现在能给中国读者写信真是我的荣幸啊。我从来没想过自己会成为作家,更没想到我的作品会流传到你们的国家,一个离我家十万八千里的地方。

当我还是个小屁孩的时候,我和我的朋友曾试着挖地洞,希望一直挖下去就能到地球另一端的中国。不一会儿,我们就放弃了这个想法（要知道,挖洞是件多辛苦的事儿啊!）;但现在通过我的这些作品,我终于到中国来了——只是通过另一种方式,跟我的想象有点不一样的方式。

谢谢你们让《小屁孩日记》在中国成为畅销书。我希望你们觉得这些故事是有趣的,也希望这些故事对你们是一种激励,让你们有朝一日也成为作家和漫画家。我是幸运的,因为我的梦想就是成为一个漫画家,而现在这个梦想实现了。不管你们的梦想是什么,我都希望你们梦想成真。

我希望有朝一日能亲身到中国看看。这是个将要实现的梦想!

希望你们喜欢《小屁孩日记》的第五册（编者注：即中译本第9、10册）。再次感谢你们对这套书的喜爱!

杰夫

A Letter to Chinese Readers

Hello to all my fans in China!

I've had a fascination with China ever since I was a boy, and it's a real privilege to be writing to you now. I never could have imagined that I would become an author, and that my work would reach a place as far from my home as your own country.

When I was a kid, my friends and I tried to dig a hole in the ground, because we hoped we could reach China on the other side of the earth. We gave up after a few minutes (digging is hard!), but with these books, I'm getting to reach your country... just in a different way than I had imagined.

*Thank you so much for making **Diary of a Wimpy Kid** a success in your country. I hope you find the stories funny and that they inspire you to become writers and cartoonists. I feel very fortunate to have achieved my dream to become a cartoonist, and I hope you achieve your dream, too... whatever it might be.*

I hope to one day visit China. It would be a dream come true!

*I hope you enjoy the fifth **Wimpy Kid** book. Thank you again for embracing my books!*

Jeff

有趣的书，好玩的书

夏致

这是一个美国中学男生的日记。他为自己的瘦小个子而苦恼，老是会担心被同班的大块头欺负，会感慨"为什么分班不是按个头分而是按年龄分"。这是他心里一道小小的自卑，可是另一方面呢，他又为自己的脑瓜比别人灵光而沾沾自喜，心里嘲笑同班同学是笨蛋，老想投机取巧偷懒。

他在老妈的要求下写日记，幻想着自己成名后拿日记本应付蜂拥而至的记者；他特意在分班时装得不会念书，好让自己被分进基础班，打的主意是"尽可能降低别人对你的期望值，这样即使最后你可能几乎什么都不用干，也总能给他们带来惊喜"；他喜欢玩电子游戏，可是他爸爸常常把他赶出家去，好让他多活动一下。结果他跑到朋友家里去继续打游戏，然后在回家的路上用别人家的喷水器弄湿身子，扮成一身大汗的样子；他眼红自己的好朋友手受伤以后得到女生的百般呵护，就故意用绷带把自己的手掌缠得严严实实的装伤员，没招来女生的关注反而惹来自己不想搭理的人；不过，一山还有一山高，格雷再聪明，在家里还是敌不过哥哥罗德里克，还是被耍得团团转；而正在上幼儿园的弟弟曼尼可以"恃小卖小"，无论怎么捣蛋都有爸妈护着，让格雷无可奈何。

这个狡黠、机趣、自恋、胆小、爱出风头、喜欢懒散的男孩，一点都不符合人们心目中的那种懂事上进的好孩子形象，奇怪的是这个缺点不少的男孩子让我忍不住喜欢他。

人们总想对生活中的一切事情贴上个"好"或"坏"的标签。要是找不出它的实在可见的好处，它就一定是"坏"，是没有价值的。单纯的有趣，让我们增添几分好感和热爱，这难道不是比读书学习考试重要得多的事情吗?! 生活就像一个蜜糖罐子，我们是趴在桌子边踮高脚尖伸出手，眼巴巴地瞅着罐子的孩子。有趣不就是蜂蜜的滋味吗?

翻开这本书后，我每次笑声与下一次笑声之间停顿不超过五分钟。一是因为格雷满脑子的鬼主意和诡辩，实在让人忍俊不禁。二是因为我还能毫不费劲地明白他的想法，一下子就捕捉到格雷的逻辑好笑在哪里，然后会心一笑。

小学二年级的时候我和同班的男生打架；初一的时候放学后我在黑板上写"某某某（男生）是个大笨蛋"；初二的时候，同桌的男生起立回答老师的提问，我偷偷移开他的椅子，让他的屁股结结实实地亲吻了地面……我对初中男生的记忆少得可怜。到了高中，进了一所重点中学，大多数的男生要么是专心学习的乖男孩，要么是个性飞扬的早熟少年。除了愚人节和邻班的同学集体调换教室糊弄老师以外，男生们很少再玩恶作剧了。仿佛大家不约而同都知道，自己已经过了有资格耍小聪明，并且要完以后别人会觉得自己可爱的年龄了。

如果你是一位超过中学年龄的大朋友，欢迎你和我在阅读时光中做一次短暂的童年之旅；如果你是格雷的同龄人，我真羡慕你们，因为你们读了这本日记之后，还可以在自己的周围发现比格雷的经历更妙趣横生的小故事，让阅读的美好体验延续到生活里。

要是给我一个机会再过一次童年，我一定会睁大自己还没有患上近视的眼睛，仔细发掘身边有趣的小事情，拿起笔记录下来。亲爱的读者，不知道当你读完这本小书后，是否也有同样的感觉?

片刻之后我转念一想，也许从现在开始，还来得及呢。作者创作这本图画日记那年是 30 岁，那么说来我还有 9 年时间呢。

一种简单的快乐

刘恺威

我接触《小屁孩日记》的时间其实并不长，是大约在一年多以前，我从香港飞回横店时，在机场的书店里看到了《小屁孩日记》的漫画。可能每一个人喜爱的漫画风格都不太一样，比如有人喜欢美式的、日系的、中国风的，有人注重写实感的，而我个人就比较偏向于这种线条简单的、随性的漫画，而且人物表情也都非常可爱。所以当时一下子就被封面吸引住了，再翻了翻内容，越看越觉得开心有趣，所以立刻就买下了它。

说实话，我并不认为《小屁孩日记》只是一本简单的儿童读物。我向别人推荐它的时候也会说，它是一本可以给大人看的漫画书，可以让整个人都感受到那种纯粹的开心。可能大家或多或少都会有这样的感受，当我们离开学校出来工作以后，渐渐的变得忙碌、和家人聚在一起的时间越来越少，也无法避免地接收到一些压力和负面情绪，对生活和社会的认知也变得更加复杂，有时候会感觉很累，心情烦躁，但如果真的自问为什么会这么累，究竟在辛苦追求着什么的时候，自己却又没有真正的答案……这并不是说我对成年后的生活有多么悲观，但像小孩子一样简单的快乐，确实离成年人越来越远了。但当我在看到《小屁孩日记》的时候，我却突然间想起了自己童年时那种纯真、简单的生活，这也是我决定买下这本漫画的原因之一。看《小屁孩日记》会让我把自己带回正轨，审核自己，检查一下自己最近的情绪、状况，还是要回到人的根本——开心。

　　我到现在也喜欢随手画一些小屁孩的画像来送给大家，这个也是最近一年来形成的习惯，因为自己大学读的是建筑，平时就喜欢随手画些东西，喜欢上小屁孩之后就开始画里面的人物，别看这个漫画线条简单，但想要用最简单的线条画出漫画里那种可爱的感觉，反而挺花功夫的。除了小屁孩这个主角之外，我最喜欢画的就是他的弟弟。弟弟是个特别爱搞鬼的小孩，而且长着一张让人特别想去捏他的脸。这兄弟俩的故事经常会让我想起我跟我妹妹的关系，我妹妹小时候也总是被我"欺负"，比如捏她的脸啊、整蛊她啊，但如果遇到了外人欺负妹妹，自己绝对是第一个站出来保护她的人。

六月

星期五

对我来说，这三个月的暑假让我于心有愧。

就因为天气晴朗，大家都指望你整天在屋外"欢蹦乱跳"。要是有一时半会你没呆在外头，别人就会想你是哪里出毛病了。可事实上我一向都喜欢呆在屋里啊。

拉上窗帘，关掉电灯，坐在电视机前打电子游戏。这才是我的暑假嘛。

唉，老妈心目中的完美假期和我想的相差十万八千里。

1

老妈说外头阳光灿烂，小孩子躲在屋里是"违背自然"的。我告诉她，我是在保护自己的皮肤，以免到了她这把岁数，脸上堆满褶子。可她一点也不想听我的解释。

老妈老想让我到外头活动活动，比方说去游泳。问题是，我已经把过半的假期耗在哥们罗利的泳池里了，情况却不大理想。

罗利一家加入了一个乡村俱乐部。学校一放暑假，我们俩天天都泡在那里。

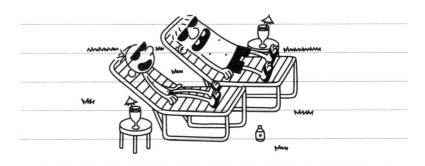

后来我们犯了一个错误——邀请刚搬进小区的女孩崔斯特一起玩。我觉得我们俩已经够意思了，愿意跟她分享乡村俱乐部的舒适生活。可是当我们仨来到泳池，她遇到一个救生员，就把我们抛诸脑后——是我们邀请她来的呀。

这回我得到的教训是，有些人可以毫不犹豫地利用你，特别是在跟乡村俱乐部有关的事情上。

话说回来，少了女生的牵绊，我和罗利四处溜达还更方便。眼下我们都是单身汉，暑假嘛，还是了无牵绊更好。

几天前，我觉察到这家乡村俱乐部的服务质量有所下降。比如说，有时候桑拿浴的温度过高，高了好几度，还有一次服务员忘了往我那杯水果沙冰放小·雨伞。

我向罗利的爸爸投诉，但不知道为什么，我的这些投诉意见杰弗逊先生半句也没向俱乐部经理反映。

这真是怪事。如果掏腰包的人是我，我一定会确保自己在乡村俱乐部得到的服务对得起我所花的钱。

没过多久，罗利就跟我说，他爸不让他再带我去游泳池了。这正合我意——呆在空调房里我更开心，而且不用每喝一口汽水都得先看看里面有没有蜜蜂。

星期六

我之前说过，老妈总想让我跟着她和我弟弟曼尼去游泳，不过我们家只能去市镇公共泳池。一旦你在乡村俱乐部享受过，就很难回到小镇的游泳池做个普通人了。

而且去年我就向自己发过誓，永远不再踏足那个地方。在公共游泳池那里，你得穿过更衣室才能走到泳池。那就是说，要经过那些男人一丝不挂地打肥皂泡的地方——淋浴区。

第一次经过男更衣室的经历，使我的心灵蒙上了巨大的阴影。

淋浴后方能进入泳池

　　我的眼睛没有瞎算幸运了。说真的，要是老爸老妈有意要让我看到这个比恐怖电影可怕一千倍的场景，干嘛还费那么大劲要我远离恐怖电影那些东西呢。

　　我真希望老妈不要再叫我去公共泳池，每回她提起这件事，我脑袋中就会重现那幅我竭力想要忘记的画面。

星期日

　　我决定了，余下的假期我要留在屋里。昨晚老妈开了一次"家庭会议"，说今年家里入不敷出，我们没钱去海边玩——这就是说家庭旅游泡汤了。

　　真恼人！我还指望这个暑假可以去海边。这倒不是因为我喜欢大海和沙子，事实上我一点都不喜欢那些玩意儿。很久之前，我就意识到全世界的鱼、乌龟和鲸鱼都在大海里大小便。不过似乎只有我被这个问题所困扰。

　　我的哥哥罗德里克喜欢捉弄我，他以为我害怕海浪。但我跟你保证，完全不是那么回事。

　　话说回来，我之所以那么期待到海边，是因为今年我终于长到可以玩"头盖骨摇晃机"的最低身高了。这个机动游戏设在人行木板道上，很刺激。罗德里克至少玩过一百次了，他口口声声说玩过这个才称得上是个男子汉。

老妈说要是我们今年"省吃俭用"，也许明年就能去海边玩了。接着她又说，不去海边也没什么，我们一家人还是能在一起尽享天伦之乐，日后我们回想起来，仍然会觉得这是"最美好的暑假"。

算了吧，这个暑假我只剩下两个寄托了：一个是我的生日，另一个是报纸的连载漫画"小·可爱"的大结局。我不记得之前有没有说过，"小·可爱"是史上最糟糕的漫画。为了让你对我的话有个直观认识，请看今天报纸上的连载：

问题是：尽管我讨厌"小·可爱"，我还是忍不住要看，老爸也一样。大概我们都想看看这漫画能有多差劲。

"小·可爱"连载了至少 30 年，作者是一个叫鲍勃·珀斯特的家伙。我听说"小·可爱"其实就是鲍勃儿子小时候的故事。

我猜，现在"小·可爱"的原型已经长大成人了，他爸爸一定为寻找新题材而大伤脑筋。

摇摇

　　几周前，报纸宣布鲍勃·珀斯特即将封笔，最后一期"小·可爱"将在八月面世。从那时起，我和老爸一直在给最后一期倒计时。

六月

　　等最后一期"小·可爱"见报，我和老爸就会开派对，这样的事情确实值得好好庆祝一番。

星期一

　　尽管我和老爸在"小·可爱"的问题上英雄所见略同，但在很多事情上我们仍然是死对头。眼下最大的分歧是我的作息时间。暑假我喜欢熬通宵看电视或打游戏，然后一觉睡到下午。可要是老爸下班回家看到我还躺在床上，他准会暴跳如雷。

最近，老爸总是在中午给我打电话，检查我是不是还在睡觉。于是我把电话放在床边，用我听起来最清醒的声音接老爸的电话。

我觉得老爸是嫉妒我们每天在家里优哉游哉，而他却要上班。

要是他真的因为这个而恼火，他应该去当一名教师或者铲雪车司机，那样就可以享受暑假了。

老妈也没让老爸好受。她每天给上班的老爸拨五个电话，事无巨细地汇报家里的最新情况。

星期二

　　母亲节那天，老爸送了老妈一架新照相机，最近几天老妈拍了很多照片。我觉得那是因为我们的家庭相册好久没有更新了，老妈有点愧疚。

　　我哥罗德里克出生后，老妈便将所有事情通通抛诸脑后。

罗德里克第一次吃豌豆

罗德里克第二次吃豌豆

罗德里克迈出第一步

砰！

　　我估计老妈生下我之后就忙不过来了，从那时起，我们家的正史就留下了大片空白。

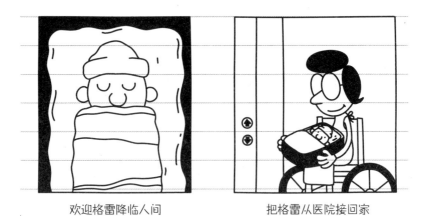

欢迎格雷降临人间 把格雷从医院接回家

格雷的6岁生日派对 格雷上中学的第一天

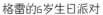

　　不过没关系，我已经明白，相片集并不能如实地记录你的人生。去年我们家到海边玩，老妈在一家纪念品商店买了一堆五彩斑斓的贝壳，然后她把贝壳埋在沙里，让曼尼去"掘宝"。

干吗要让我看见这一幕呢，这让我要重新打量自己的童年。

格雷真的"挖到"贝壳了！

今天老妈说我看起来"蓬头垢脸"，她要带我去剪头发。

要是我知道老妈带我去的地方是她和外婆经常光顾的"丽人美发店"，打死我也不跟她到那儿去剪头发。

不过我得说，这次去美发店倒不太糟糕。首先，那儿到处都有电视机，可以一边等发型师一边看节目。

其次，那儿有很多小报，就是那些人们在超市一边排队等候结账一边看的报纸。老妈说小报充斥着谎言，可我觉得小报上确实有些重要的东西。

尽管老妈不喜欢小报，但外婆还是经常买。几个星期前外婆好几天不接电话，老妈心急火燎地开车去外婆家，却发现她好得很。她不接电话全因她读到的一段新闻。

老妈问外婆，她是怎么知道这条信息的，外婆说：

外婆养的狗亨利最近死了，所以外婆多出很多空闲时间。于是最近一段时间老妈经常要处理无绳电话之类的事情。

只要老妈在外婆家发现小报的踪影，马上就会把报纸带回家，扔进垃圾桶。上周我在垃圾桶里翻到一张小报，偷偷拿回房里看。

我很庆幸自己读了这张小报。报上说北美大陆六个月后就会被水淹没，这样一来我就没必要在学校里好好学习了。

所以我并不介意在美发店里等很久。在那儿我可以读到自己的星相图，看到电影明星没化妆的样子，又怎么会觉得无聊呢？

轮到我剪头发的时候，我才发现美发店最妙的地方——八卦。美发店的女职员知道镇上每个人的破事儿。

唉，帕帕斯先生和小他二十岁的新太太的故事我才听到一半，老妈就来接我走了。

要是我的头发长得快一点就好了，我就可以回来继续听完整个故事。

星期五

我觉得老妈开始后悔前几天带我去丽人美发店剪头发。那里的女职员把肥皂剧介绍给我，现在我已经深陷其中不能自拔。

昨天的肥皂剧我正看到一半，老妈就命令我关上电视机，找点别的事情做。我知道没有讨价还价的余地，就叫罗利来我家玩。

罗利一到，我们直奔罗德里克的房间，他的房间在地下室。罗德里克和他的"水不湿乐队"到外面排练，每次他一走我就去翻他的东西，看看能不能找到些有趣的玩意。

我曾经翻出一个钥匙圈，上面吊着一幅小小的旅游纪念画。这是我在罗德里克抽屉的垃圾堆里所找到的最好的东西。

要是你往里面看，就会看到一张罗德里克和某个女生的合照。

我不晓得罗德里克是怎么拍到那张照片的，每次家庭旅游我都和他一起，要是我看到他和那个女孩在一起，我一定会记得她的。

我把照片递给罗利看，鉴于他一脸猴急的样子，我得自己拿着钥匙圈，免得被他一手抢走。

我们又四处翻箱倒柜，在罗德里克的抽屉里我们找到一盘恐怖电影的光碟。我们的运气好得令人难以置信。我和罗利谁也没看过恐怖电影，这算得上是大收获了。

我问老妈罗利能不能在我们家留宿，她说没问题。我特意等老爸不在房间的时候才去问老妈，他不喜欢我在"工作日的晚上"留同学在我们家过夜。

去年暑假罗利也在我们家留宿过，我们一起睡地下室。

我让罗利在正对锅炉房的床上睡，因为我特别害怕那房间。万一三更半夜鬼魂从那儿飘出来，它会先抓住罗利，我就多了五秒钟的时间逃跑。

凌晨一点左右，我们听见锅炉房里有些动静，吓得魂飞魄散。

那声音听起来像一个年幼的女鬼，它说：

我和罗利没命地冲上楼梯，几乎没把对方给踩死。

我们冲进老爸老妈的房间，我跟他们说我们的房子有鬼，必须马上搬家。

20

看起来老爸并不相信我的话，他下楼到地下室，径直走进锅炉房。我和罗利躲在十尺开外的地方。

我敢说老爸十有八九没命活着走出那房间。里面传出一阵沙沙声，又发出几声砰砰声，我已经准备好拔腿就跑。

但不一会儿，老爸拿着一个叫"躲猫猫的哈利"的玩偶走了出来，那是曼尼的玩具。

昨晚我和罗利等老爸老妈睡着之后，就开始看我们从罗德里克那里翻出的电影。实际上，只有我一个人在看，因为罗利几乎整部电影都捂着自己的眼睛和耳朵。

　　电影说的是一只泥手的故事，它到处游走杀人。看到这只手的人就是下一个受害者。

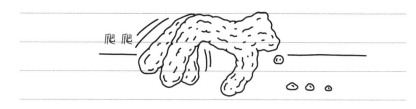

　　电影的特效很假，我从头看到尾，一点都不觉得害怕。然而意想不到的事情发生了。

　　泥手掐死了最后一个人，就朝着屏幕方向爬，然后屏幕就黑了。起初我还有点摸不着头脑，没多久我反应过来了：下一个受害者，就是我。

　　我关上电视机，把整个故事从头到尾跟罗利讲了一遍。

哈，我肯定讲得不错，因为罗利听完故事显然比我还害怕。

这次我们不能再去老爸老妈的房里避难了，要是他们知道我们看恐怖片，准会罚我禁闭在家。可是地下室让人感觉很不安全，于是我们整夜都呆在楼上的浴室，把电灯全打开。

要是我们能够整夜不睡就好了。第二天早上，老爸在浴室发现了我们，那个场面可真够难看的。

　　老爸问我们是怎么回事，我只好从实招来。老爸把事情告诉老妈，所以现在我能做的就是等着老妈说要关我多长时间禁闭。不过说句实话，比起老妈炮制的惩罚措施，我更担心泥手的事情。

　　还好，有一点对我稍有安慰——我发现泥手每天只能爬行一小段路。

　　但愿泥手真如我想的一样，那我就能多一点活命的时间。

星期二

昨天，老妈又给我说教了，说像我这么大的男孩，看那么多暴力电影，打那么多电子游戏，都不知道什么活动才是真正的娱乐。

我一声不吭地听着，因为我不知道她说这些话，下一步是要干什么。

老妈接着说，她准备为住在附近的男孩组织一个"读书俱乐部"，由她来教我们欣赏那些我们有眼不识的文学名著。

我赶紧向老妈讨饶，求她按平日那样罚我在家禁闭好了。可她不为所动。

今天是"悦读"俱乐部第一次活动。一众男孩慑于母亲们的压力来到现场，我为此感到内疚。

悦读

还好老妈没有邀请弗雷格。弗雷格就是那个住在街北边的怪小孩。最近他的举止比平日更加古怪。

想听听我的"卫生问题"吗？

我慢慢觉得弗雷格是个危险人物，幸好他整个暑假都没有离开他家的院子。他爸妈准是给自家院子围上了电栅栏之类的东西。

回到正题，老妈叫我们带上自己最喜欢的书来参加今天的活动，我们可以从中选一本来讨论。大家都把自己的书摊在桌上。这些书让大家都兴高采烈的，独独老妈例外。

26

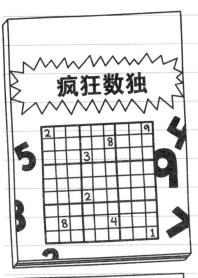

老妈说我们带的这些书都不是"真正的"文学作品，我们得从"经典名著"起步。

说着她拿出几本书，一看就知道这些书的年纪快赶上老妈了。

这不就是老师在课堂老逼着我们看的那种书嘛！

学校有个读书计划，要是你在课余时间读了一本"经典名著"，老师会奖励你一个汉堡包图案的贴纸。

你说他们想糊弄谁呢。在楼下的手工店花五毛钱就可以买到一百个这样的贴纸。

我不大清楚什么样的书才算是"经典名著"，不过我觉得它至少得上五十岁，而且结局得有人或者动物死了。

老妈说，我们要是不喜欢她挑的书，可以去一趟图书馆，一起挑一本大家都喜欢的。我可不想去那个地方。

跟你坦白说吧，八岁那年我去图书馆借了一本书，后来我把这事全忘了。过了几年我在书桌后面找到那本书，那时候我算过自己大概得付图书馆两千块钱滞纳金。

于是我把书藏在衣柜那个放旧漫画书的盒子里，至今它还在那里。从那时候起我再没踏足过图书馆半步，可我心里明白，一旦我出现，就是自投罗网。

事实上，我一见到图书馆管理员就紧张得大汗淋漓。

我问老妈能不能再给一次机会让我们自己挑书，她批准了。我们明天再碰头，把自己第二次挑的书带过来。

星期三

你看吧，这一夜过后"悦读"俱乐部就受到了重创。昨天来的人今天大部分都没有再出现，只剩我跟罗利了。

罗利带来了两本书。

我挑的书是"魔法和怪兽：黑暗领域"系列的第九集。我想老妈应该会喜欢吧，这故事又长，又没有多少插图。

可老妈一点也不喜欢我的书。她说她不喜欢封面插图那种描绘女性的手法。

我读过《魔法和怪兽》，我记得故事里压根没有女性角色。我真有点怀疑封面插图的作者有没有读过这本书。

说回选书，老妈说她要行使她作为"悦读"俱乐部创始人的一票否决权，亲自为我们选择一本书。她选的是《夏洛的网》—— 一眼看上去就知道还是我之前说的那种"经典名著"。

光看封面就知道，这女孩和猪准有一个活不到故事的结尾。

星期五

呵呵，最后"悦读"俱乐部只剩一个会员了，那就是我。

昨天不知道罗利和他爸是去打高尔夫球还是干别的什么，总之他就是扔下我见死不救。我没有做老妈布置的阅读作业，还指望着他来掩护我的呀。

没有完成阅读作业真不是我的错。昨天老妈要我在自己的房间里读二十分钟的书，可要我这么长时间地集中注意力的确是个大问题啊。

我玩得正投入，却被老妈逮住了，她说我不读完那本书就别想看电视。所以昨天晚上我得等她睡了才能补上我的娱乐时间。

可那部电影中的泥手还在我的脑海里挥之不去。要是我一个人在深夜里看电视，泥手会不会从沙发下爬出来，一把拽住我的腿或什么地方……我越想越害怕。

于是我在地上铺了一排衣服，沿着走廊从我的卧室一直铺到客厅去，这样问题就解决了。

我上楼下楼都不会碰到地板。

今天早上我放在楼梯口的字典绊倒了老爸，所以现在他恨我恨得牙痒痒的。不过我宁愿挑别的日子来惹老爸生气。

只是我又担心，那只泥手会趁我睡着了爬上床来抓住我。这几天睡觉时我都用被子捂住整个身体，只留一个洞用来呼吸。

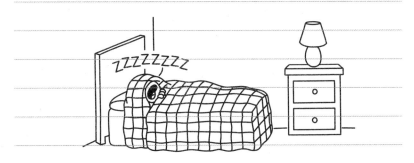

34

但这个方法也有它的风险。罗德里克今天进了我房间，我费了一早上功夫才把嘴巴里那股臭袜子的味道洗干净。

星期日

今天是我读完《夏洛的网》前三章的最后期限。老妈知道我不能完成任务，就说我们一起坐在饭桌前读书，直到我读完为止。

过了半小时，前门传来敲门声，是罗利来了。我还以为他是回来参加"悦读"俱乐部的，不过一看到他爸爸也一道过来了，我就知道准没好事。

杰弗逊先生手里拿着一张看起来很正式的纸，上面印着乡村俱乐部的标志。他说这是我和罗利在俱乐部吃水果沙冰的账单，总额是83美元。

那几次我和罗利在俱乐部点单，每次都在账单上签上杰弗逊先生的客户代码。没人跟我们说过那些账单是要付钱的。

我还搞不懂杰弗逊先生来我家要干吗。我一直觉得他是建筑设计师之类的人物，要是他缺这83块钱，只要多设计一栋房子就可以了。可他还是跟老妈谈了一阵子，他们一致同意让我和罗利自己掏钱买单。

我跟老妈说，我和罗利只是小屁孩，我们都没有工作没有工资。可老妈说我们得有"创意"。接着她说在我们还清自己的欠款之前，"悦读"俱乐部的活动会暂停。

实话跟你说，听到这话我松了一口气。这个时候，只要是与读书没有关系，什么事情都好说。

星期二

我和罗利昨天冥思苦想了一整天，看看怎么做才能还掉那93块钱。罗利要我去自动柜员机取钱还给他爸爸就行了。

罗利说这话，是因为他以为我是阔少。几年前，罗利放假来我家玩，不巧家里的厕纸用完了，老爸又没空去超市购买日用品，我们家就用这种餐巾纸暂时凑合着。

罗利一定是以为这种餐巾纸是一种高档的厕纸，他还问我们家是不是家财万贯。

我当然不会放过这个让他崇拜我的机会。

但话说回来，我压根没多少钱，坏就坏在这了。我翻来覆去地想，一个像我这么大的小孩能从哪里捞到几张票子呢。突然灵感来了：我们可以提供草坪维护服务。

我说的不是那种普普通通的草坪维护服务。我说的是一家能让你的草坪更上一层楼的公司。我们为公司取名为"VIP草坪服务"。

我们打电话给电话黄页公司的人，说我们想在黄页上登一则广告。不是那种小豆腐块式的文字广告，而是一张跨页全彩印的大幅广告。

但黄页公司的职员告诉我们，登那种广告得花好几千块钱。

我跟他们说，这太不讲理了，别人一毛钱都还没赚到，又怎么拿得出广告费呢？

我和罗利意识到我们得另觅出路，自己做广告。

我们可以制作宣传单，贴到附近每家每户的信箱上。我们只需要找到一些现成的剪贴画就可以开工了。

于是我们去街角的小·店买了一张卡片，女生都喜欢拿这些卡片当生日贺卡送给别人。

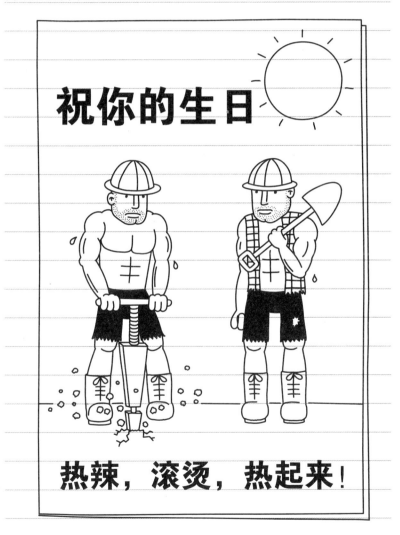

然后我们把卡片扫描进罗利的电脑里，把我俩的头像 PS 在卡片的人身上。

接着我们复制了一些修草坪的工具，粘贴在卡片上。最后打印出来。我得说，这张宣传单看上去棒极了。

VIP
草坪服务

我们提供获奖无数、世界级别的服务，

让你和你的草坪都尽情放松一下吧！

请致电 555-2941

我算了一笔帐，如果要打印数量足够在整个社区张贴的宣传单，我们得花几百块买彩色墨盒和打印纸。于是我们向罗利的爸爸提议，不如由他去超市替我们买这些东西。

杰弗逊先生可不买我们的帐。更糟的是，他还禁止我们使用他的电脑，也不许我们用电脑打印传单。

这让我着实吃了一惊。是他要我们还他钱的啊，他就不应该给我们添堵。不过我们也只能拿着刚才打印出来的那张传单，离开了他的办公室。

我和罗利逐家逐户拍门，向人们展示我们的传单，宣传我们的 VIP 草坪服务。

走访了几家之后，我们发现了一条捷径：让看了我们传单的人把传单传给下一个人看，这样一个传一个，我和罗利就既可以省下传单，也可以省下跑腿的功夫了。

现在我们只需要安坐家中等待电话滔滔而来。

星期四

我和罗利昨天等了一整天，一个电话都没接到。

我开始琢磨我们是不是要再找一张印着更多肌肉男的卡片，重新制作宣传单。

今天早上十一点左右，我们终于接到甘菲尔太太的电话，她和我外婆住在同一条街上。她说她家的草坪需要请人修剪，不过她要求有人来证明我们的工作能力，才会雇用我们。

我曾经给外婆打理过草坪，于是我打电话给她，请她打电话给甘菲尔太太，好让甘菲尔太太知道我有多么能干。

唉，我准是选错了打电话的日子，因为外婆把我痛骂了一顿。她说去年秋天我在她家草坪上留下一堆堆的枯叶，弄得现在她的院子里到处是一小块一小块的枯草。

然后她问我什么时候去她那里收拾残局。

我要的可不是这样的回复。我跟外婆说，眼下我们只进行有偿服务，收拾残局的事也许到暑假晚点的时候我们可以再和她联系。

我打电话给甘菲尔太太，尽我最大努力模仿外婆的声线。幸好我还没有到变声期。

VIP草坪服务公司按我的要求打理好草坪，他们的服务好极了。

你还别不信，甘菲尔太太上钩了。她谢过"外婆"，就挂了电话。几分钟之后她的电话来了，这回我用自己的声音接电话。甘菲尔太太说她准备请我们干活，要我们今天晚点时候去她家开始工作。

可我家离甘菲尔太太家有点远，我问甘菲尔太太能不能开车来接我们过去。她似乎很不高兴我们没有自备交通工具，不过她还是说，如果我们可以中午出发，她就可以顺道载我们过去。

中午十二点，甘菲尔太太开着她儿子的小货车来到我家门口，一见面她就问我们的割草机和其他工具在哪里。

我说我们其实没有任何工具，不过我外婆从来不锁房子的后门，我可以偷偷溜进去，借她的割草机用几个小时。看来甘菲尔太太非常急于修剪自家的草坪，因为她居然没有反对我的计划。

44

还好外婆不在家，我轻而易举地就把割草机从她的屋里弄出来了……我们把机器推到甘菲尔太太的院子里，准备动手干活。

　　就在这个时候，我和罗利才意识到我和他谁也没有用过割草机。我们俩围着割草机研究了半天，谁也没搞懂怎么开动这个玩意。

戳 戳

　　倒霉的事还在后头，我们拨弄割草机的时候，一不小心把汽油全撒到草坪上了。我们只好回外婆家取汽油给割草机加油。

　　我拿起割草机的使用手册，睁大眼睛去读。谁知手册上全是西班牙语。从我勉强能理解的零碎语句来看，使用割草机比我原来想的要危险得多。

PRECAUCIÓN!
El uso incorrecto
puede tener como
resultado graves
lesiones fisicas o
muerte.

Siempre
conserve los
pies y las manos
alejadas de las
cuchillas del
cortacésped.

Nunca utilice el
cortacésped
durante
tempestades
con truenos.

我跟罗利说，可以先由他割草，而我就坐在树荫下，谋划我们下一步的赚钱大计。

罗利一点也不买我的帐。他说这是一盘"合伙"生意，每件事情大家都要各做一半。他的话让我很惊讶，因为我才是那个想出割草服务主意的人，按理说我应该是雇主，而不是合伙人。

我跟罗利说，我们之中得有个人干粗活，另外一个人收钱，这样子钞票就不会被汗弄得粘糊糊的。

信不信由你，听我这么一说，罗利居然撒手不干了。

我先把话说在前头，要是罗利以后找工作的时候需要我做推荐人，我一定会给他一个差评。

我其实不需要罗利。如果这门割草生意按照我的设想发展，会有一百个像罗利这样的人投到我门下。

　　不过这个时候，我需要给甘菲尔太太割草。我又仔细看了一阵子使用手册，终于弄明白要发动割草机得拉下那个由一根绳索系着的把手。我就照着做了。

　　割草机立马动起来，我推着它来回跑动。

　　割草没有我之前想的那么辛苦。割草机自带动力驱动，我要做的就是跟在它的屁股后面，每隔一会儿就让它拐个弯。

　　这时候我看到草坪上到处是一砣一砣的狗屎。要让一部自带驱动的割草机及时绕过狗屎，可不是件容易的事。

拐弯

VIP草坪服务公司有一条关于狗屎的严格规定：我们绝不靠近狗屎。

所以我一看到疑似狗屎的物体，就立马推着割草机绕它画一个直径十英尺的圆圈，以策万全。

这样一来，我完成任务的速度就快得多，因为需要割草的地方少了。完工以后，我到甘菲尔太太家的门前收钱。账单总共是三十块，其中二十块是割草坪的费用，另外十块用来补偿我和罗利设计传单花费的时间和精力。

可甘菲尔太太不肯付钱。她说我们的服务"糟糕透了"，我们几乎没怎么动过她的草坪。

我告诉她狗屎的事情，可她还是不肯交出欠我的钱。更糟糕的是，连载我回家也不愿意了。我知道做生意也许会遇到别人赖账，可我万万没有想到这个人会是我们的第一个顾客。

我只好走路回家，到家的时候我生气极了，就把整个故事原原本本告诉老爸，说我如何做起割草生意，甘菲尔太太如何不肯付钱。

老爸立马开车到甘菲尔太太家，我赶紧跟着他。我以为他会狠狠骂对方从自己儿子身上捞好处，我想在现场亲眼见证这一幕。可是老爸只是从外婆的屋子里拿来割草机，把甘菲尔太太的草坪修剪干净。

割完草后他甚至没有找甘菲尔太太要钱。

这一趟出门完全是浪费时间。趁老爸在收拾东西，我在甘菲尔太太的前院竖了一块牌子。

如果没什么指望收到钱的话，给自己做个免费广告也好，就当是对我劳动的补偿。

星期六

VIP 草坪服务公司并没有如我所想那样发展起来。第一单生意过后我再也没接到活了，我开始怀疑甘菲尔太太最近是不是跟她的邻居说过我的坏话。

我考虑过收手不干，但随即意识到，只要稍微修改一下传单，冬天一到我们又可以从头再来了。

VIP
铲雪服务

试过那么多家
还选我们这家!

现在问题是，我需要钱。我打电话叫罗利想想新点子，她妈妈说他跟他爸看电影去了。我有点恼火，因为他根本没来问我一下就跑去休假了。

在我付清水果沙冰的账单前，老妈是不会允许我去玩的。这就是说，我得想法子赚到这笔钱。

让我来告诉你谁是有钱人吧，曼尼。我的意思是，那小孩富得很。几周前老妈和老爸跟他约定，如果曼尼不用他们督促就主动用座便器，尿尿一次他们就给曼尼 25 美分。所以现在曼尼总是拉着几升水到处走。

曼尼把钱全放在一个大的广口瓶里，瓶子放在他的衣橱上。那里面至少有 150 块钱。

我考虑过向曼尼借钱，可就是拉不下面子开口。而且我很肯定曼尼会收利息。

　　我在盘算着怎么样才能不用干活就挣到钱。老妈听完我的想法，说我不过是"懒"嘛。

　　好吧，也许我确实是懒，但这并不是我的错。打小时候起我就是这么懒。要是有人早点教育我把我纠正过来，也许我就不会长成现在这个样子了。

　　我还记得上学前班的时候，游戏时间一结束，老师就会叫大家收拾好玩具，我们一边放玩具、一边唱"收拾歌"。歌是和大家一起唱的，不过收拾玩具的事情我几乎没怎么干过。

如果你想找人为我现在这副模样负责，我觉得你应该首先找公共教育体制算帐。

星期天

老妈今天早上进来叫我起床做礼拜。我乐意至极，因为我知道我得向更高层次的力量求助，才能付清水果沙冰的账单。不管外婆需要什么她都会祈祷，很快她就能得偿所愿。

我觉得她一定有一条直线电话直通上帝那儿。

由于某些原因我并没有这样的门路。不过这不等于说我会放弃尝试。

敬爱的主，请您让杰弗逊先生撞到头，那样他就会忘了我欠他的钱。也请您让我顺利通过古怪巫师游戏的第三关，无需使用额外的补血道具。阿门。提前感谢您！

今天的布道词的主题是"乔装的耶稣"，说的是你应该善意对待遇到的每个人，因为你永远不会知道哪个人是乔装打扮的耶稣。

我觉得布道词的目的是让你成为一个更善良的人，不过它只会让我变成妄想狂，因为我知道我一定会猜错。

哇，谢谢你帮我擦亮皮鞋！

弗雷德，不用客气！

这时候教堂里的人跟往常一样传递着捐献箱。我唯一的想法是，不管是谁收到这些钱，我都比他更需要这笔钱。

老妈准是看到我的眼神，因为我还没来得及拿走我需要的东西，她就把捐献箱传给后排的人了。

星期一

这个周末就是我的生日，我总是等不及这姗姗来迟的生日。今年我要举行一个家庭派对。对于罗利擅自退出草坪维护生意的行为我还耿耿于怀，所以我不想给他错觉，让他以为可以来我家吃生日蛋糕。

另外，对朋友派对的事我已经吃一堑长一智。参加朋友派对的客人都以为他们可以对你收到的礼物为所欲为。

每回我举行朋友派对，老妈总是邀请她朋友的孩子来，结果我要和一堆素未谋面的小孩一起庆生。

那些小孩都不会自己挑礼物给我，礼物都是他们的母亲选的。尽管你能收到电子游戏之类的东西，但绝对不会是你想玩的那一款。

小青蛙和小狗

学会分享

我还是庆幸这个暑假不用参加游泳队。去年我生日那天要训练，老妈在泳池边让我下车。

于是那次我挨了无数老拳，游泳的时候连手臂都抬不起来。

所以说到庆祝生日，我的经验是最好把小·孩什么的排除在考虑范围之外。

老妈说只要我不像"往常那样"对待收到的生日贺卡，就可以搞一场家庭派对。真烦人，我本来自创了一套了不起的方法处理贺卡。我把贺卡整整齐齐码成一叠，然后逐张打开，把夹在中间的钞票甩下来。只要我不去看贺卡的内容，就可以在一分钟之内处理完二十张贺卡。

摇 摇

老妈说我在"侮辱"那些送我贺卡的人。她说这一次我得逐一打开贺卡看上面的内容，并且向送卡者致谢。那样子会降低我的工作效率，不过我觉得这还是值得的。

最近我一直在想，今年生日我该要些什么礼物。我最想要一条狗。

过去三年我一直问家人要一只小狗，可老妈说我们要等曼尼学会自己用马桶了才能养小狗。哼，看曼尼学用马桶家里闹得鸡飞狗跳那样子，就知道他永远都学不会。

关键是，我知道老爸也想养条狗。他小时候养过。

我想老爸是需要一点推动力。去年的圣诞节我眼看着机会要来了。我的叔叔乔和他的妻儿来我们家做客，顺便也带上他们的小狗奇勒。

我问乔叔叔能不能给老爸一点暗示，让他也给我们买只小狗。不过乔叔叔帮了倒忙，令我的计划进度倒退了五年。

另一件我心仪的生日礼物就更不用指望了，那就是手机。这个结局全拜罗德里克所赐。

老妈老爸去年送了一台手机给罗德里克，第一个月他就用了三百块钱话费。大部分电话是罗德里克打给老爸老妈，叫他们去去打开地下室的暖气。

所以今年我要的礼物是一张豪华皮革躺椅。查理叔叔有一张，他基本上是躺在上面过日子的。

要是我有躺椅，每天深夜看完电视后就不用上楼去房里睡觉了，直接在躺椅上睡就行。这是我想要躺椅的主要原因。

另外，躺椅有各种功能，比如说脖子按摩和硬度调节之类的。我觉得"震动"功能在老爸讲大道理的时候可以让时间过得快一些。

有了躺椅，我唯一需要起身去做的事就是上洗手间。不过也许我想等明年再问家人要躺椅吧，我敢说厂家明年会研究出新型号可以解决上洗手间的问题。

星期二

尽管我的头发还用不着修剪，今天我还是叫老妈带我去丽人美发店。我心痒痒要去听镇上最新鲜的八卦。

我的理发师安奈特说，她从一位认识杰弗逊太太的女士那里听说，我和罗利闹别扭了。

显然，因为我没有邀请他来参加我的生日派对，罗利心都碎了。哼，说是说罗利心里难过，但你从他脸上根本看不出来。

每次我看到罗利，他总是跟屁虫似的和他爸爸形影不离。在我看来，他已经给自己找到一个新的好朋友。

我只想说，罗利明明有份欠着水果沙冰的账单，还可以经常去乡村俱乐部玩，这让我很不爽。

倒霉的是，罗利和他爸爸的亲密关系逐渐影响到我的生活。老妈说，罗利和他爸爸在一起玩"好得很"，我和老爸也应该一起活动活动，比如去钓鱼或者在前院玩接球游戏什么的。

不过问题是，我和老爸都不是那种搞父子活动的料。老妈上次让我和老爸一起玩，结果是我不得不把老爸从拉帕汉诺克河里救上来。

老妈不死心。她说想看到老爸和我们几个孩子之间有更多"温情"。这么搞法有时只会让人感到尴尬。

① 英语中"蹲下"和"鸭子"是同一个单词，格雷爸爸以为格雷在告诉他河里有鸭子。

星期五

今天，正当我在电视机前自娱自乐的时候，前门传来一阵敲门声。老妈说有位"朋友"来看望我，我想一定是罗利上门向我请罪来了。

可敲门的不是罗利。是弗雷格。

我大吃一惊，一回过神，就马上甩手把门关上了。关上门后我感到害怕，天晓得弗雷格在我家前门干吗。几分钟过后，我透过侧面的窗子往外看：弗雷格依然站在那里。

我知道自己得采取一些有力的措施，于是我走进厨房，打电话报警。可我还没按完"911"三个键，老妈就阻止了我。

老妈说是她邀请弗雷格来的。她说我和罗利吵架之后，看起来"形单影只"，于是她为我和弗雷格创造了一次"一起玩"的机会。

看到了吧，这就是我从来不把自己的私事告诉老妈的原因。这个弗雷格事件简直是场灾难。

我听说，吸血鬼只有在你邀请它来的时候才能进入你的屋子里。我敢说弗雷格也是这样的。

所以现在我担心的事情总共有两件：泥手和弗雷格。要是让我选哪一样先找到我，我会马上选泥手。

星期六

今天是我的生日，事情或多或少按我的预想发展。下午一点左右亲戚一个个到了。我叫老妈能请多少人来就请多少人来，那我就可以收到最多礼物，结果相当理想。

过生日的时候我喜欢一步到位直奔礼物环节。所以我叫大家在客厅里集合。

按照老妈吩咐，我用了足够的时间处理贺卡。这有一点痛苦，不过我收获甚丰，倒还算值得。

倒霉的是，一看到我开始把钞票从贺卡里抽出来，老妈就把钱全部没收，说要还给杰弗逊先生。

接着是包装好的礼物，不过数量不多。第一件礼物是老爸老妈送的，体积小·重量大，我以为这是个好兆头。不过打开礼物的时候我依然吃了一惊。

甲壳虫小·姐
蜂窝移动电话
给小·孩和老人的完美礼物！

再仔细一点看，我发现那并不是平日所见到的手机。这个玩意叫"甲壳虫小·姐"，上面并没有键盘之类的输入设备。上面只有两个按钮：一个按钮是拨回家，一个按钮是拨紧急呼叫。所以这手机基本没啥用。

其他礼物还包括衣服和一些我不需要的东西。我还盼着也许会收到躺椅，不过当我意识到屋里没有地方可以让老爸老妈藏起这么一件庞然大物的时候，我也就死心了。

接着老妈跟大家说该到饭厅吃蛋糕了。倒霉的是，乔叔叔的狗奇勒比我们抢先一步。

咕噜咕噜
啧啧

我本来希望老妈会上街给我买个新蛋糕，可她只是拿把小刀切掉狗咬过的那部分蛋糕。

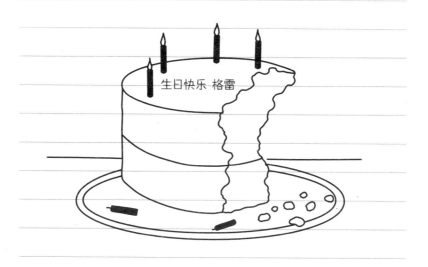

生日快乐 格雷

老妈给我切了一大块蛋糕，可到这个时候我真的没心情吃蛋糕，尤其是我看到奇勒在桌底吐出生日蜡烛时，就更不用说了。

星期天

我想老妈为我的生日落得这个下场感到难过，因为今天她说我们可以去购物广场买一件礼物补偿。

老妈带上曼尼和罗德里克，她说他们也可以各自挑件礼物。这一点都不公平，昨天又不是他们过生日。

我们在购物广场逛了一圈，脚步最后停在一家宠物店。我巴望着大家一起凑钱买只小狗，但罗德里克似乎对另外一种宠物更感兴趣。

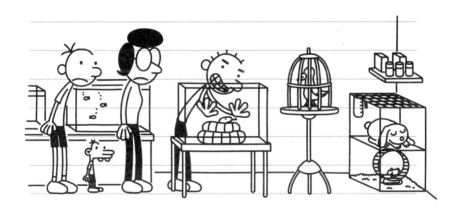

老妈给我们每人 5 块钱，让我们想要啥就买啥。可是 5 块钱在宠物店里能买什么呢。我的目标最后锁定了一条长得很帅的神仙鱼，它身上有各种颜色。

　　罗德里克选的也是鱼。我不知道他选的是什么鱼。罗德里克买它是因为贴在水族箱上的标签说这条鱼"富有攻击性"。

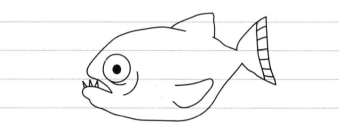

　　曼尼的5块钱全买了鱼饲料。起初我以为他想用这饲料喂我和罗德里克的鱼。不过等我们回到家，我发现曼尼已经吃掉了半盒饲料。

星期一

　　这是我第一次拥有自己的宠物，我有点爱上它了。我每天喂三次鱼，把小鱼缸刷得干干净净。

我还写了一本养鱼日记，每天记录鱼的一举一动。不过我得承认，我开始觉得填满一页日记有点困难。

我问老爸老妈可不可以买一个水族箱，再买一堆鱼给我的小家伙做伴。可老爸说水族箱很贵，也许到了圣诞节我可以要水族箱做礼物吧。

看到了吧，这就是做小孩吃亏的地方。每年你只有两次机会可以得到你想要的东西，那就是圣诞节和你的生日。等这两个日子真的到来，你父母就把事情搞砸，给你买一个"甲壳虫小姐"。

要是我自己有钱，就可以想要什么就买什么，省得每次我想租一盘游戏碟或者买一块糖果的时候都要丢脸。

不管怎么说，我知道自己以后一定会名利双全。不过我有点担心，为什么到现在还没有什么苗头。我觉得到现在我至少应该有一档自己的电视真人秀节目。

昨天晚上我一直看电视真人秀，说的是有个保姆和一个家庭同住一周，逐样逐样指出那一家人如何把家里弄得乱七八糟。

不知道那位女士是不是上过什么保姆特殊培训班，不过我天生就是做这种工作的料子。

这个保姆迟早会退休不干，我现在要做的就是搞清楚怎么才能进入保姆的候补人选名单。

几年前我开始收集自己的个人物品，比如读书报告、旧玩具之类。日后我的博物馆开业，我希望里面满是自己生活中有趣的东西。

不过我没有保存沾有我口水的棒棒糖棍子之类的东西，我又不需要克隆自己的后代。

等我成了名人，我就要改变一下自己的生活方式。

我大概只能坐私人飞机，因为坐普通航班的话，人们总是要分享我所在的头等舱的洗手间。

名人不得不处理的另一件事是——他们年幼的弟妹也跟着鸡犬升天，而这只是因为他们有血缘关系。

迄今，我最接近出名机会的一次是几年前老妈替我报名做平面模特儿。我估计她打的算盘是让我的照片出现在邮购目录之类的东西上面。

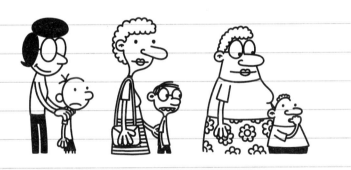

但我的照片只是被用在这本无聊的医药书封面上。我一直努力洗脱自己的嫌疑。

星期二

整个下午我都在打游戏，看周日连载漫画。

我翻到封底，往常刊载"小可爱"的位置登了一则广告。

> 希望你的作品出现在幽默版上吗？
> 我们正在寻找一位有才华的漫画作者为我们创作单格漫画，以填补"小可爱"留下的空缺。你能逗我们发笑吗？
> 以动物或宠物为题材的漫画恕不考虑。

天啊，我一直苦苦等待的不就是这个机会嘛。我曾经在校报上发表过一期漫画，这次可是我声名鹊起的大好机会。

广告商说他们不接受关于动物的漫画，我认为我知道其原因。有部漫画叫"宝贝狗狗"已经连载了差不多50年。

漫画的作者离世很久了，不过报纸还在重复登载着他的旧作。

我不知道这部漫画好不好笑，说句实话，像我这么大的孩子都觉得大部分狗狗漫画不知道说些什么。

话又说回来，有几次报纸都想停掉"宝贝狗狗"的连载，不过每次他们停掉这部漫画，不知从哪儿全都冒出来的漫画迷就会大吵大闹。我想人们大概是把这只漫画狗当成自家宠物了。

上一次报纸停掉"宝贝狗狗"，报社的办公楼门口连续来了四辆公共汽车，上面全是从老人活动中心过来的老人。他们一直堵在报社门口，直到报社答应他们的要求后才离开。

TO JONATHAN

DIARY
of a
Wimpy Kid

(7)

by Jeff Kinney

JUNE

<u>Friday</u>

For me, summer vacation is basically a three-month guilt trip.

Just because the weather's nice, everyone expects you to be outside all day "frolicking" or whatever. And if you don't spend every second outdoors, people think there's something wrong with you. But the truth is, I've always been more of an indoor person.

The way I like to spend my summer vacation is in front of the TV, playing video games with the curtains closed and the lights turned off.

Unfortunately, Mom's idea of the perfect summer vacation is different from mine.

Mom says it's not "natural" for a kid to stay indoors when it's sunny out. I tell her that I'm just trying to protect my skin so I don't look all wrinkly when I'm old like her, but she doesn't want to hear it.

Mom keeps trying to get me to do something outside, like go to the pool. But I spent the first part of the summer at my friend Rowley's pool, and that didn't work out so good.

Rowley's family belongs to a country club, and when school let out for the summer, we were going there every single day.

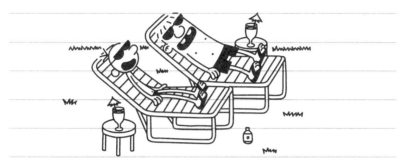

Then we made the mistake of inviting this girl named Trista who just moved into our neighborhood. I thought it would be really nice of us to share our country club lifestyle with her. But five seconds after we got to the pool, she met some lifeguard and forgot all about the guys who invited her there.

The lesson I learned is that some people won't think twice about using you, especially when there's a country club involved.

Me and Rowley were better off without a girl hanging around, anyway. We're both bachelors at the moment, and during the summer it's better to be unattached.

A few days ago I noticed the quality of service at the country club was starting to go down a little. Like sometimes the temperature in the sauna was a few degrees too hot, and one time the poolside waiter forgot to put one of those little umbrellas in my fruit smoothie.

I reported all my complaints to Rowley's dad. But for some reason Mr. Jefferson never passed them on to the clubhouse manager.

Which is kind of weird. If it was me who was paying for a country club membership, I'd want to make sure I was getting my money's worth.

Anyway, a little while later Rowley told me he wasn't allowed to invite me to his pool anymore, which is fine with ME. I'm much happier inside my air-conditioned house, where I don't have to check my soda can for bees every time I go to take a sip.

Saturday

Like I said, Mom keeps trying to get me to go to the pool with her and my little brother, Manny, but the thing is, my family belongs to the TOWN pool, not the country club. And once you've tasted the country club life, it's hard to go back to being an ordinary Joe at the town pool.

Besides, last year I swore to myself that I would never go back to that place again. At the town pool you have to go through the locker room before you can go swimming, and that means walking through the shower area, where grown men are soaping down right out in the open.

The first time I walked through the men's locker room at the town pool was one of the most traumatic experiences of my life.

I'm probably lucky I didn't go blind. Seriously, I don't see why Mom and Dad bother to try and protect me from horror movies and stuff like that if they're gonna expose me to something about a thousand times worse.

I really wish Mom would stop asking me to go to the town pool, because every time she does, it puts images in my mind that I've been trying hard to forget.

Sunday

Well, now I'm DEFINITELY staying indoors for the rest of the summer. Mom had a "house meeting" last night and said money is tight this year and we can't afford to go to the beach, which means no family vacation.

THAT really stinks. I was actually looking FORWARD to going to the beach this summer. Not because I like the ocean and the sand and all of that, because I don't. I realized a long time ago that all the world's fish and turtles and whales go to the bathroom right there in the ocean. And I seem to be the only person who's bothered by this.

My brother Rodrick likes to tease me because he thinks I'm afraid of the waves. But I'm telling you, that's not it at all.

Anyway, I was looking forward to going to the beach because I'm finally tall enough to go on the Cranium Shaker, which is this really awesome ride that's on the boardwalk. Rodrick's been on the Cranium Shaker at least a hundred times, and he says you can't call yourself a man until you ride it.

Mom said maybe if we "save our pennies" we can go back to the beach next year. Then she said we'd still do a lot of fun stuff as a family and one day we'll look back on this as the "best summer ever".

Well, now I only have two things to look forward to this summer. One is my birthday, and the other is when the last "Li'l Cutie" comic runs in the paper. I don't know if I ever mentioned this before, but "Li'l Cutie" is the worst comic ever. To give you an idea of what I'm talking about, here's what ran in the paper today —

Daddy, is rain just God sweating?

But here's the thing: Even though I hate "Li'l Cutie," I can't stop myself from reading it, and Dad can't, either. I guess we just like seeing how bad it is.

"Li'l Cutie" has been around for at least thirty years, and it's written by this guy named Bob Post. I've heard Li'l Cutie is based on Bob's son when he was a little kid.

But I guess now that the real Li'l Cutie is all grown up, his dad's having trouble coming up with new material.

A couple of weeks ago the newspaper announced that Bob Post is retiring and the final "Li'l Cutie" is gonna be printed in August. Ever since then me and Dad have been counting down the days until the last comic runs.

When the last "Li'l Cutie" comes out, me and Dad will have to throw a party, because something like that deserves a serious celebration.

Monday

Even though me and Dad see eye to eye on "Li'l Cutie," there are still a lot of things we butt heads over. The big issue between us right now is my sleep schedule. During the summer I like to stay up all night watching TV or playing video games and then sleep through the morning. But Dad gets kind of crabby if I'm still in bed when he gets home from work.

Lately, Dad's been calling me at noon to make sure I'm not still asleep. So I keep a phone by my bed and use my best wide-awake voice when he calls.

I think Dad's jealous because he has to go to work while the rest of us get to kick back and take it easy every day.

But if he's gonna be all grumpy about it, he should just become a teacher or a snowplow driver or have one of those jobs where you get to take summers off.

Mom's not really helping improve Dad's mood, either. She calls him at work about five times a day with updates on everything that's going on around the house.

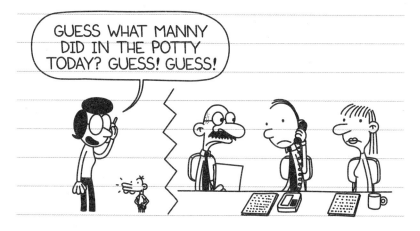

GUESS WHAT MANNY DID IN THE POTTY TODAY? GUESS! GUESS!

Tuesday
Dad got Mom a new camera for Mother's Day, and lately she's been taking lots of pictures. I think it's because she feels guilty about not keeping up on the family photo albums.

When my older brother, Rodrick, was a baby, Mom was totally on top of things.

Rodrick's first time trying peas

Rodrick's second time trying peas

Rodrick's first steps

Kaboom!

Once I came along I guess Mom got busy, so from that point on there are a lot of gaps in our official family history.

Welcome Gregory
to the world

Taking Gregory home
from the hospital

Gregory's 6th
birthday party

Gregory's first
day of middle school

I've learned that photo albums aren't an accurate
record of what happened in your life, anyway.
Last year when we were at the beach, Mom
bought a bunch of fancy seashells at a gift shop,
and later on I saw her bury them in the sand
for Manny to "discover".

Well, I wish I didn't see that, because it made me re-evaluate my whole childhood.

Gregory really "digs" seashells!

Today Mom said I was looking "shaggy", so she told me she was taking me to get a haircut.

But I never would've agreed to get my hair cut if I knew that Mom was taking me to Bombshells Beauty Salon, which is where Mom and Gramma get THEIR hair cut.

I have to say, though, the whole beauty salon experience wasn't that bad. First of all, they have TVs all over the place, so you can watch a show while you're waiting to get your hair cut.

Second, they have lots of tabloids, those newspapers you see in the checkout lines at grocery stores. Mom says tabloids are full of lies, but I think there's some really important stuff in those things.

Gramma is always buying tabloids, even though Mom doesn't approve. A few weeks ago Gramma wasn't answering her phone, so Mom got worried and drove over to Gramma's to see if she was OK. Gramma was fine, but she wasn't picking up her phone because of something she read.

But when Mom asked Gramma where she got her information, Gramma said —

UM... THE NEW YORK TIMES.

Gramma's dog, Henry, died recently, and ever since then Gramma has had a lot of time on her hands. So Mom's dealing with stuff like the cordless phone thing a lot these days.

Whenever Mom finds any tabloids at Gramma's house, she takes them home and throws them in the garbage. Last week I fished one out of the trash and read it in my bedroom.

I'm glad I did. I found out that North America will be underwater within six months, so that kind of takes the pressure off me to do well in school.

I had a long wait at the beauty salon, but I didn't really mind. I got to read my horoscope and look at pictures of movie stars without their makeup, so I was definitely entertained.

When I got my hair cut, I found out the best thing about the beauty salon, which is the GOSSIP. The ladies who work there know the dirt on just about everyone in town.

Unfortunately, Mom came to pick me up right in the middle of a story about Mr. Peppers and his new wife, who's twenty years younger than him.

Hopefully my hair will grow out fast so I can come back and hear the rest of the story.

Friday
I think Mom's starting to regret taking me to get my hair cut the other day. The ladies at Bombshells introduced me to soap operas, and now I'm totally hooked.

Yesterday I was in the middle of my show, and Mom told me I had to turn off the TV and find something else to do. I could tell there was no use arguing with her, so I called Rowley and invited him over.

When Rowley got to my house, we went straight to Rodrick's room in the basement. Rodrick is off playing with his band, Löded Diper, and whenever he's away I like to go through his stuff and see if I can find anything interesting.

The best thing I found in Rodrick's junk drawer this time around was one of those little souvenir picture keychains you get at the beach.

If you look into it, you see a picture of Rodrick with some girl.

I don't know how Rodrick got that picture, because I've been with him on every single family vacation, and if I saw him with THAT girl, I definitely would have remembered her.

I showed the picture to Rowley, but I had to hold the keychain because he was getting all grabby.

We dug around some more, and then we found a
horror movie at the bottom of Rodrick's drawer.
I couldn't believe our luck. Neither one of us had
actually seen a horror movie before, so this was a
really big find.

I asked Mom if Rowley could spend the night,
and she said yes. I made sure I asked Mom when
Dad was out of the room, because Dad doesn't like
it when I have sleepovers on a "work night".

Last summer Rowley spent the night at my
house, and we slept in the basement.

I made sure Rowley took the bed that was closest to the furnace room, because that room really freaks me out. I figured if anything came out of there in the middle of the night, it would grab Rowley first and I'd have a five-second head start to escape.

At about 1:00 in the morning, we heard something in the furnace room that scared the living daylights out of us.

It sounded like a little ghost girl or something, and it said —

Me and Rowley practically trampled each other to death trying to get up the basement stairs.

We burst into Mom and Dad's room, and I
told them our house was haunted and we had
to move immediately.

Dad didn't seem convinced, and he went down to
the basement and walked right into the furnace
room. Me and Rowley stayed about ten feet back.

I was pretty sure Dad wasn't going to get out
of there alive. I heard some rustling and a few
bumps, and I was ready to make a run for it.

THUNK
WHUMP

But a few seconds later he came back out with one of Manny's toys, a doll named Hide-and-Seek Harry.

Last night me and Rowley waited for Mom and Dad to go to bed, and then we watched our movie. Technically, I was the only one who watched it, because Rowley had his eyes and ears covered the whole entire time.

The movie was about this muddy hand that goes around the country killing people. And the last person who sees the hand is always the next victim.

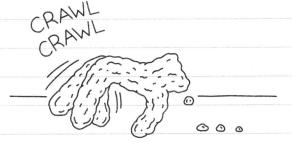

CRAWL
CRAWL

The special effects were really cheesy, and I wasn't even scared until the very end. That's when the twist came.

After the muddy hand strangled its last victim, it came crawling straight at the screen, and then the screen went black. At first I was a little confused, but then I realized it meant the next victim was gonna be ME.

I turned the TV off, and then I described the whole movie to Rowley from beginning to end.

Well, I must've done a pretty good job telling the story, because Rowley got even more freaked-out than I was.

I knew we couldn't go to Mom and Dad this time because they'd ground me if they found out we watched a horror movie. But we didn't feel safe in the basement, so we spent the rest of the night in the upstairs bathroom with the lights on.

I just wish we had managed to stay awake the whole night, because when Dad found us in the morning, it wasn't a pretty scene.

Dad wanted to know what was going on, and I had to fess up. Dad told Mom, so now I'm just waiting to hear how long I'm gonna be grounded for. But to be honest with you, I'm a lot more worried about this muddy hand than any punishment Mom can dream up.

I thought about it, though, and I realized there's only so much ground a muddy hand can cover in a day.

So hopefully that means I have a little while longer to live.

Tuesday

Yesterday, Mom lectured me about how boys my age watch too many violent movies and play too many video games, and that we don't know what REAL entertainment is.

I just stayed quiet, because I wasn't sure exactly where she was going with all this.

Then Mom said that she was gonna start a "reading club" for the boys in the neighborhood so she could teach us about all the great literature we were missing out on.

I begged Mom to just give me a regular punishment instead, but she wouldn't budge.

So today was the first meeting of the Reading Is Fun Club. I felt kind of bad for all the boys whose moms made THEM come.

READING IS FUN

I was just glad Mom didn't invite Fregley, this weird kid who lives up the street, because he's been acting stranger than usual lately.

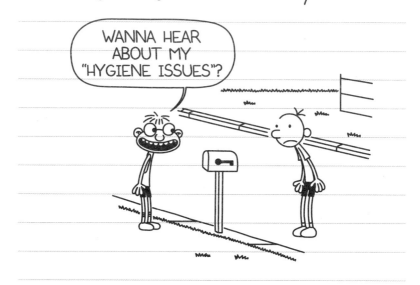

I'm starting to think maybe Fregley's a little dangerous, but luckily he doesn't really leave his front yard during the summer. I think his parents must have an electrical fence or something.

Anyway, Mom told everyone to bring their favorite book to today's meeting so we could pick one and discuss it. All the guys laid their books on the table, and everyone seemed pretty happy with the selection except Mom.

Mom said the books we brought weren't "real" literature and that we were gonna have to start with the "classics."

Then she brought out a bunch of books that she must've had since SHE was a kid.

These are the exact same types of books our teachers are always pushing us to read at school.

They have a program where if you read a "classic" in your free time, they reward you with a sticker of a hamburger or something like that.

I don't know who they think they're fooling. You can get a sheet of a hundred stickers down at the arts-and-crafts store for fifty cents.

I'm not really sure what makes a book a "classic" to begin with, but I think it has to be at least fifty years old and some person or animal has to die at the end.

Mom said if we didn't like the books she picked out, we could go on a field trip to the library and find something we all agreed on. But that won't work for me.

See, when I was eight years old I borrowed a book from the library, and then I forgot all about it. I found the book a few years later behind my desk, and I figured I must've owed about two thousand dollars in late fees on that thing.

So I buried the book in a box of old comics in my closet, and that's where it is to this day. I haven't been back to the library since then, but I know if I ever DO show up, they'll be waiting for me.

In fact, I get nervous if I even SEE a librarian.

I asked Mom if we could get a second chance to pick out a book on our own, and she said we could. We're supposed to meet again tomorrow and bring our new selections with us.

Wednesday
Well, the membership of the Reading Is Fun Club took a big hit overnight. Most of the guys who came yesterday bailed out, and now there's only two of us.

Rowley brought two books along with him.

The book I picked was the ninth volume in the "Magick and Monsters: Dark Realms" series. I figured Mom would like it because it's pretty long and there aren't any pictures.

But Mom didn't like my book. She said she didn't approve of the illustration on the cover because she didn't like the way it portrayed women.

I've read "Shadowdoom," and from what I can remember, there aren't even any women in the story. In fact, I kind of wonder if the person who designed the cover even READ the book.

Anyway, Mom said that she was gonna use her veto power as the Reading Is Fun Club's founder and choose the book for us. So she chose this book called "Charlotte's Web," which looks like one of those "classics" I was talking about before.

Just from looking at the cover, I guarantee either the girl or the pig doesn't make it to the end of the book.

Friday
Well, the Reading Is Fun Club is down to one member, and that's me.

Yesterday Rowley went golfing or something with his dad, so he kind of hung me out to dry. I didn't do my reading assignment, and I was really counting on him to cover for me at the meeting.

It's not really my fault that I couldn't finish my reading assignment, though. Mom told me I had to read in my bedroom for twenty minutes yesterday, but the truth is, I just have trouble concentrating for long periods of time.

After Mom caught me horsing around, she banned me from watching TV until I read the book. So last night I had to wait until she went to bed before I could get my entertainment fix.

I kept thinking about that movie with the muddy hand, though. I was afraid that if I was watching TV all by myself late at night, the muddy hand might crawl out from under the couch and grab my foot or something.

The way I solved the problem was by making a trail of clothes and other stuff all the way from my bedroom down to the family room.

That way I was able to make it downstairs and back without ever touching the ground.

This morning Dad tripped over a dictionary I left at the top of the stairs, so now he's mad at me. But I'll take Dad being angry over the alternative any day of the week.

My new fear is that the hand is gonna crawl up on my bed and get me in my sleep. So lately I've been covering my whole body with the blanket and leaving a hole so I can breathe.

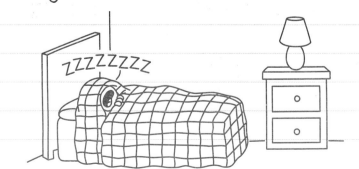

But that strategy has its OWN risks. Rodrick got into my room today, and I had to spend the morning trying to wash the taste of a dirty sock out of my mouth.

Sunday

Today was my deadline for finishing the first three chapters of "Charlotte's Web." When Mom found out I wasn't done yet, she said we were gonna sit down at the kitchen table until I was finished.

READING IS FUN

About a half hour later there was a knock at the front door, and it was Rowley. I thought maybe he was coming back to the Reading Is Fun Club, but when I saw that his dad was with him, I knew something was up.

Mr. Jefferson had an official-looking piece of paper with the country club logo on it. He said it was a bill for all the fruit smoothies me and Rowley ordered at the clubhouse, and the grand total was eighty-three dollars.

All those times me and Rowley ordered drinks at the clubhouse, we just wrote down Mr. Jefferson's account number on the tab. Nobody told us someone actually had to PAY for all that.

I still didn't really understand what Mr. Jefferson was doing at MY house. I think he's an architect or something, so if he needs eighty-three bucks, he can just design an extra building. He talked to Mom, though, and they both agreed that me and Rowley needed to pay off the tab.

I told Mom me and Rowley are just kids and it's not like we have salaries or careers or whatever. But Mom said we were just gonna have to be "creative." Then she said we would have to suspend the Reading Is Fun Club's meetings until we paid what we owed.

To be honest with you, I'm kind of relieved. Because at this point, anything that doesn't involve reading sounds pretty good to me.

Tuesday

Me and Rowley racked our brains all day yesterday trying to figure out how to pay off that eighty-three dollars. Rowley said maybe I should just go to the ATM and withdraw some money to pay off his dad.

The reason Rowley said that is because he thinks I'm rich. A couple of years ago during the holidays, Rowley came over and we had just run out of toilet paper at my house. My family was using these holiday cocktail napkins as a substitute until Dad got to the store again.

Rowley thought the holiday napkins were some kind of really fancy toilet paper, and he asked me if my family was rich.

I wasn't gonna pass up the opportunity to impress him.

Anyway, I'm NOT rich, and that's the problem. I tried to figure out a way a kid my age could get his hands on some cash, and then it hit me: We could start a lawn care service.

I'm not talking about some average, run-of-the-mill lawn care service, either. I'm talking about a company that takes lawn care to the next level. We decided to name our company the V.I.P. Lawn Service.

We called up the Yellow Pages people and told them we wanted to place an ad in their book. And not just one of those tiny little text ads, but a really big one with full color that takes up two whole pages.

But get this: The Yellow Pages people told us it was gonna cost us a few thousand bucks to put our ad in their book.

I told them that didn't make a lot of sense to me, because how's someone supposed to pay for an ad if they haven't even earned any money yet?

Me and Rowley realized we were gonna have to do this a different way, and make our OWN ads.

I figured we could just make flyers and put them in every mailbox in our neighborhood. All we needed was some clip art to get us started.

So we went down to the corner store and bought one of those cards women get each other on their birthdays.

Then we scanned it into Rowley's computer and pasted pictures of OUR heads onto the bodies from the card.

After that we got some clip art of lawn tools and put it all together. Then we printed it out, and I have to say, it looked great.

I did some math, and I figured it would cost us at least a couple hundred bucks in color ink cartridges and paper to make enough flyers for the whole neighborhood. So we asked Rowley's dad if he'd go out to the store and get us all the stuff we needed.

Mr. Jefferson didn't go for it. In fact, he told us we couldn't use his computer or print out any more copies of our flyer.

I was a little surprised by that, because if Mr. Jefferson wanted us to pay him back, he sure wasn't making it easy. But all we could really do was take our one flyer and get out of his office.

Then me and Rowley went around from house to house showing everyone our flyer and telling them about the V.I.P. Lawn Service.

After we hit a few houses, we realized it would be a lot easier to just ask the next person we spoke with to pass the flyer along so me and Rowley wouldn't have to do all that walking.

Now the only thing we have to do is sit back and wait for the phone calls to start rolling in.

Thursday
Me and Rowley waited around all day yesterday, but we didn't get any calls.

I was starting to wonder if we should try to find a card with more muscular guys for our next flyer. Then, at about 11:00 this morning, we got a call from Mrs. Canfield, who lives on Gramma's street. She said her lawn needed mowing but she wanted to check our references before she hired us.

I used to do lawn work for Gramma, so I called her up and asked if she could call Mrs. Canfield and tell her what a good worker I am.

Well, I must've caught Gramma on a bad day, because she really lit into me. She said I left piles of leaves on her lawn last fall and now there were patches of dead grass all over her yard.

Then she asked me when I was gonna come over and finish the job.

That was not really the kind of response I was looking for. I told Gramma we were only taking paying jobs at the moment but maybe we could get back to her later on in the summer.

Then I called Mrs. Canfield and did my best imitation of Gramma. I guess I'm lucky my voice hasn't changed yet.

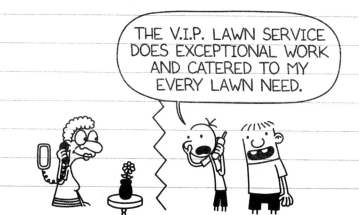

THE V.I.P. LAWN SERVICE DOES EXCEPTIONAL WORK AND CATERED TO MY EVERY LAWN NEED.

Believe it or not, Mrs. Canfield bought it. She thanked "Gramma" for the reference and hung up. Then she called back a few minutes later, and I answered in my regular voice. Mrs. Canfield said she'd hire us and that we should come by her house later today to get started.

But it's kind of far from my house to Mrs. Canfield's, so I asked her if she could come get us. She didn't seem real happy that we didn't have our own transportation, but she said she'd be willing to pick us up if we could be ready at noon.

Mrs. Canfield came to my house at 12:00 in her son's pickup truck, and she asked us where our lawn mower and all our equipment was.

I said we didn't actually HAVE any equipment but that my Gramma keeps her side door unlocked and I might be able to sneak in and borrow her mower for a few hours. I guess Mrs. Canfield must have been pretty desperate to get her lawn mowed, because she went along with my plan.

Luckily, Gramma wasn't home, so it was easy to get the mower out of her house. We rolled it over to Mrs. Canfield's yard, and then we were ready to get to work.

That's when me and Rowley realized neither one of us had ever actually operated a lawn mower before. So the two of us poked around for a while and tried to figure out how to get the thing started.

Unfortunately, when we tilted the mower on its side, all the gasoline spilled out onto the grass, and we had to go back over to Gramma's to get a refill.

I picked up the owner's manual for the mower while we were at it. I tried to read it, but the instructions were written in Spanish. I got the feeling from the bits and pieces I COULD understand that operating a lawn mower was a lot more dangerous than I originally thought.

PRECAUCIÓN!
El uso incorrecto puede tener como resultado graves lesiones físicas o muerte.

Siempre conserve los pies y las manos alejadas de las cuchillas del cortacésped.

Nunca utilice el cortacésped durante tempestades con truenos.

I told Rowley he could have the first crack at
the lawn mowing and that I would go sit in the
shade and start working on our business plan.

Rowley didn't like that idea at all. He said this
was a "partnership" and that everything had to
be 50-50. I was pretty surprised by this, because
I'm the one who came up with the idea for the
lawn service in the first place, so I was more like
the owner than a partner.

I told Rowley we needed someone to do the grunt
work and someone to handle the money so it didn't
get all sweaty.

Believe it or not, that was enough to make Rowley
walk right off the job.

I just wanna say for the record that if Rowley ever needs me for a job reference in the future, I'm gonna have to give him a lousy review.

The truth is, I don't really need Rowley anyway. If this lawn service business grows the way I think it will, I'm gonna have about a HUNDRED Rowleys working for me.

In the meantime, I needed to get Mrs. Canfield's lawn mowed. I looked through the manual for a little while longer and then figured out that I needed to pull on this handle attached to a cord, so I tried that.

The mower started up right away, and I was off and running.

It wasn't as bad as I thought it was gonna be. The lawn mower was self-propelled, so all I needed to do was walk behind it and steer every once in a while.

Then I started to notice that there were piles of dog poop everywhere. And steering around them was not an easy thing to do with a self-propelled mower.

The V.I.P. Lawn Service has a very strict policy when it comes to dog poop, which is that we won't go anywhere near it.

So from that point on, whenever I saw anything that looked suspicious, I would mow a ten-foot circle around it just to be safe.

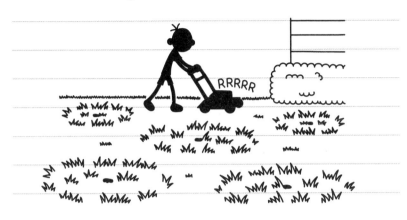

The job actually went a lot faster after that because I had a lot less lawn to cover. After I was done, I went to the front door to collect my money. The final bill was thirty dollars, which was twenty dollars for the lawn plus ten bucks for the time me and Rowley spent designing that flyer.

But Mrs. Canfield wouldn't pay. She said our service was "lousy" and that we hardly mowed any of her lawn.

I told her about the dog poop issue, but she still wouldn't cough up what she owed me. And to make matters worse, she wouldn't even give me a ride home. You know, I figured someone might try to stiff us this summer, but I never thought it would be our very first customer.

I had to walk home, and by the time I got to my house, I was really mad. I told Dad the whole story about my lawn mowing experience and how Mrs. Canfield wouldn't pay me.

Dad drove right over to Mrs. Canfield's house, and I went with him. I thought he was gonna chew her out for taking advantage of his son, and I wanted to be there to see it firsthand. But Dad just got Gramma's mower and cut the rest of Mrs. Canfield's grass.

When he was done, he didn't even ask her for any money.

The trip wasn't a TOTAL waste of time, though. When Dad wrapped things up, I planted a sign in Mrs. Canfield's front yard.

I figured if I wasn't gonna get paid, I might as well get some free advertising for all my trouble.

Saturday

The V.I.P. Lawn Service has not really panned out the way I thought it would. I haven't had any work since that first job, and I'm starting to think maybe Mrs. Canfield has been bad-mouthing me to her neighbors.

I thought about just giving up and closing our business, but then I realized that with a few tweaks to the flyer, we could start things back up again in the winter.

V.I.P. SNOW REMOVAL

YOU'VE TRIED THE REST, NOW GO WITH THE BEST!

The problem is, I need money NOW. I called up Rowley to start brainstorming new ideas, but his mom said he was at the movies with his dad. I was a little annoyed, because he never bothered to ask me if he could take the day off.

Mom's not letting me do anything fun until this fruit smoothie bill is paid off, so that meant it was up to ME to figure out how to earn the cash.

I'll tell you who has a lot of money, and that's Manny. I mean, that kid is RICH. A few weeks ago Mom and Dad told Manny they'd give him a quarter for every time he uses the potty without being asked. So now he carries around a gallon of water with him at all times.

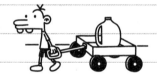

Manny keeps all his money in a big jar on his dresser. He's gotta have at least $150 in that thing.

I've thought about asking Manny to lend me the money, but I just can't bring myself to do that. I'm pretty sure Manny charges interest on his loans anyway.

I'm trying to figure out a way to earn money without doing any actual work. But when I told Mom what I was thinking, she said I'm just "lazy."

OK, so maybe I AM lazy, but it's not really my fault. I've been lazy ever since I was a little kid, and if someone had caught it early on, maybe I wouldn't be the way I am now.

I remember in preschool, when playtime was over, the teacher would tell everyone to put away their toys, and we would all sing the "Cleanup Song" while we did it. Well, I sang the song with everyone else, but I didn't do any of the actual cleaning.

So if you want to find somebody to blame for the way I am, I guess you'd have to start with the public education system.

Sunday

Mom came into my room this morning and woke me up for church. I was glad to go, because I knew I was gonna have to turn to a higher power to get this fruit smoothie bill paid off. Whenever Gramma needs anything she just prays, and she gets it right away.

I think she has a direct pipeline to God or something.

For some reason I don't have that same kind of pull. But that doesn't mean I'm gonna quit trying.

Today's sermon was called "Jesus in Disguise," and it was about how you should treat everyone you meet with kindness because you never know which person is really Jesus pretending to be someone else.

I guess that's supposed to make you wanna be a better person, but all it does is make me paranoid because I know I'm gonna just end up guessing wrong.

They passed the donation basket around like they do every week, and all I could think was how I needed that money a lot more than whoever it was going to.

But Mom must've seen the look in my eye, because she passed the basket to the row behind us before I could take what I needed.

Monday

My birthday's coming up this weekend, and it can't get here quick enough for me. This year I'm gonna have a FAMILY party. I'm still really burned up with Rowley for bailing out on our lawn care business, so I don't want him thinking he can come over and eat my birthday cake.

Plus, I've learned my lesson about friend parties. When you have a friend party, all your guests think they have the right to play with your presents.

And every time I have a friend party, Mom invites HER friends' kids, so I end up with a bunch of people at my party I barely even know.

And those kids don't buy the gifts, their MOMS do. So even if you get something like a video game, it's not a video game you'd actually want to play.

I'm just glad I'm not on the swim team this summer.
Last year I had practice on my birthday, and Mom
dropped me off at the pool.

I got so many birthday noogies that I couldn't
even lift my arms to swim.

So when it comes to your birthday, I've learned it's best to just keep kids out of the equation.

Mom said I could have a family party as long as I promised not to do my "usual" with the birthday cards. That stinks, because I have a GREAT system for opening cards. I put them all in a neat pile, and then I rip each one open and shake it to get the money out. As long as I don't stop to read anything, I can get through a pile of twenty cards in under a minute.

Mom says the way I do it is "insulting" to the people who got me the cards. She says this time around I have to read every card and acknowledge the person who gave it to me. That'll slow me down, but I guess it's still worth it.

I've been doing a lot of thinking about what I want for my birthday this year. What I REALLY want is a dog.

I've been asking for a dog for the past three years, but Mom says we have to wait until Manny's completely potty trained before we get one. Well, with the potty training racket Manny's got going on, that could take FOREVER.

The thing is, I know that Dad wants a dog, too. He used to have one when HE was a kid.

I figured all Dad needed was a little nudge, and on Christmas last year I saw my chance. My Uncle Joe and his family stopped by our house, and they brought their dog, Killer, with them.

I asked Uncle Joe if he wouldn't mind hinting to Dad that he should get us a dog. But the way Uncle Joe did it probably set my dog-getting campaign back by five years.

The other thing I have no chance of getting for my birthday is a cell phone, and I can thank Rodrick for that.

Mom and Dad got Rodrick a cell phone last year, and he racked up a bill for three hundred dollars in the first month. Most of THAT was from Rodrick calling Mom and Dad from his room in the basement to ask them to turn the heat up.

So the only thing I'm asking for this year is a deluxe leather recliner. My Uncle Charlie has one, and he practically LIVES in that thing.

The main reason I want my own recliner is because if I had one, I wouldn't have to go up to my room after watching TV late at night. I could just sleep right in the chair.

Plus, these recliners have all sorts of features, like a neck massager and adjustable firmness and stuff like that. I figure I could use the "vibrate" feature to make Dad's lectures a lot more tolerable.

The only reason I'd ever need to get up is to go to the bathroom. But maybe I should just wait until next year to ask for a recliner, because I bet they'll have that taken care of in the new model.

Thursday

I asked Mom to take me back to Bombshells Beauty Salon again today, even though I didn't really need a haircut. I just felt like catching up on the town gossip.

Annette, my hairstylist, said she heard from a lady who knows Mrs. Jefferson that me and Rowley had a falling out.

Apparently, Rowley's "heartbroken" because I didn't invite him to my birthday party. Well, if Rowley's upset, you wouldn't know it from looking at him.

Every time I see Rowley, he's palling around with his dad. So the way it looks to me, he's already got himself a new best friend.

I just wanna say I think it stinks that Rowley gets to go to the country club even though he still owes money on that fruit smoothie bill.

Unfortunately, Rowley's chummy relationship with his dad is starting to affect MY life. Mom says the way Rowley and his dad hang out together is "neat" and that me and Dad should go fishing or play catch in the front yard or something.

But the thing is, me and Dad just aren't cut out for that kind of father-son stuff. The last time Mom tried to get me and Dad to do something like that together, it ended with me having to pull him out of Rappahannock Creek.

Mom won't let it go, though. She says she wants to see more "affection" between Dad and us boys. And that's created some really awkward moments.

<u>Friday</u>

Today I was watching TV, minding my own
business, when I heard a knock at the front
door. Mom said there was a "friend" there to
see me, so I thought it must be Rowley coming
to apologize.

But it wasn't Rowley. It was FREGLEY.

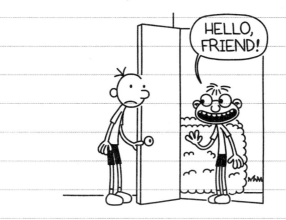

After I recovered from my initial shock, I
slammed the door shut. I started to panic because
I didn't know what Fregley was doing at my
front door. After a few minutes went by, I
looked out the side window, and Fregley was
STILL standing there.

I knew I had to take drastic measures, so I
went to the kitchen to call the cops. But Mom
stopped me before I could finish dialing 911.

Mom said SHE invited Fregley over. She said I've
seemed "lonely" ever since I had that fight with
Rowley, and she thought she'd set up a "playdate"
with Fregley.

See, this is why I should never tell Mom about my personal business. This Fregley thing was a total disaster.

I've heard that a vampire can't come inside your house unless you invite him in, and I'll bet it's the same kind of deal with Fregley.

So now I've got TWO things to worry about: the muddy hand and Fregley. And if I had to choose the one to get me first, I'd take the muddy hand in a heartbeat.

Saturday

Today was my birthday, and I guess things went more or less like I expected. The relatives started showing up around 1:00. I asked Mom to invite as many people as possible so I could maximize my gift potential, and I got a pretty good turnout.

I like to cut to the chase on my birthday and get right to the gifts, so I told everyone to gather in the living room.

I took my time with the cards, just like Mom asked. It was a little painful, but I got a good haul, so it was worth it.

A special greeting
And a "how do you do?"
For a special nephew —
By golly, that's you!

Happy
Birthday!

aunt Brenda

WOW, AUNT BRENDA, THIS IS REALLY NEAT!

WHEN I SAW IT IN THE STORE, I KNEW IT WAS JUST PERFECT!

Unfortunately, as soon as I collected my checks, Mom confiscated the money to pay off Mr. Jefferson.

PLUCK

Then I moved on to the wrapped presents, but there weren't a whole lot of those. The first gift, from Mom and Dad, was small and heavy, which I thought was a good sign. But I was still pretty shocked when I opened it.

When I looked more closely, I found out it wasn't an ordinary cell phone. It was called a "Ladybug". The phone didn't have a keypad on it or anything. It only had two buttons: one to call home and one for emergencies. So it's pretty much useless.

All my other gifts were clothes and other stuff I didn't really need. I was still hoping I might get that recliner, but once I realized there weren't any places Mom and Dad could be hiding a giant leather chair, I gave up looking.

Then Mom told everyone it was time to go into the dining room to have some cake. Unfortunately, Uncle Joe's dog, Killer, had beaten us to it.

I was hoping Mom would go out and get me a new cake, but she just took a knife and cut away the parts the dog didn't touch.

Mom cut me a big piece, but by that point I wasn't really in the mood for cake. Especially not with Killer throwing up little birthday candles under the table.

Sunday

I guess Mom must've felt bad about how my birthday went down, because today she said we could go to the mall and get a "makeup gift."

Mom took Manny and Rodrick along for the ride, and she said they could each pick out something, too, which is totally unfair, because it wasn't THEIR birthday yesterday.

We walked around the mall for a while and ended up in a pet store. I was hoping we could pool our money to buy a dog, but Rodrick seemed to be interested in a different kind of pet.

Mom handed us each a five-dollar bill and told us we could buy whatever we wanted, but five bucks doesn't exactly get you very far in a pet store. I finally settled on this really cool angelfish that's all different colors.

Rodrick picked out a fish, too. I don't know what kind it was, but the reason Rodrick chose it was because the label on the tank said the fish was "aggressive".

Manny spent HIS five bucks on fish food. At first I thought it was because he wanted to feed the fish that me and Rodrick bought, but by the time we got home, Manny had eaten half the canister.

Monday
This is the first time I've had my very own pet, and I'm kind of getting into it. I feed my fish three times a day, and I keep his bowl really clean.

I even bought a journal so I could keep track of everything my fish does during the day. I have to admit, though, I'm starting to have a little trouble filling up the pages.

I asked Mom and Dad if we could buy one of those aquariums and get a ton of fish to keep my little guy company. But Dad said that aquariums cost money and maybe I could ask for one for Christmas.

See, this is what stinks about being a kid. You only get two shots at getting stuff you want, and that's on Christmas and your birthday. And then when one of those days DOES come, your parents mess things up and buy you a Ladybug.

If I had my own money, I could just buy whatever I wanted and not have to embarrass myself every time I needed to rent a video game or buy a piece of candy or something.

Anyway, I've always known that I'll eventually be rich and famous, but I'm starting to get a little concerned that it hasn't happened yet. I figured I'd at LEAST have my own reality TV show by now.

Last night I was watching one of those television shows where a nanny lives with a family for a week and then tells them all the ways they're screwing up.

Well, I don't know if the woman had to go to some special nanny school or something, but that's the kind of job I was BORN to do.

I just need to figure out how to get myself in line for that job when the nanny retires.

YOUR HOUSE IS A WRECK, YOUR KIDS HAVE NO MANNERS, AND...HEY, MR. JOHNSON, YOU'RE NOT GOING OUT IN THAT SHIRT, ARE YOU?

A few years ago I started collecting my personal mementos, like book reports and old toys and stuff like that, because when my museum opens I wanna make sure it's packed with interesting things from my life.

But I don't keep anything like lollipop sticks that have my saliva on them because, believe me, I do NOT need to be cloned.

When I'm famous, I'm gonna have to make some life changes.

I'll probably have to fly in private jets, because if I fly on regular planes, I'll get really annoyed when people in the back try to mooch off my first-class bathroom.

Another thing famous people have to deal with is that their younger siblings end up getting famous just because they're related.

My closest brush with fame so far was when Mom signed me up for a modeling job a few years ago. I think her idea was to get pictures of me in clothes catalogues or something like that.

But the only thing they used my picture for was this stupid medical book, and I've been trying to live it down ever since.

Tuesday
I spent the afternoon playing video games and catching up on the Sunday comics.

I turned to the back page, and there was an ad where "Li'l Cutie" usually is.

Man, I've been waiting FOREVER for an opportunity like this. I had a comic in my school paper once, but this is a chance to hit the BIG time.

The ad said they weren't accepting any animal comic strips, and I think I know why. There's this comic about a dog called "Precious Poochie", and it's been running for about fifty years.

The guy who wrote it died a long time ago, but they're still recycling his old comics.

184

I don't know if they're funny or not because, to be honest with you, most of them don't even make sense to a person my age.

Anyway, the newspaper has tried to get rid of that comic a bunch of times, but whenever they try to cancel it all the "Precious Poochie" fans come out of the woodwork and make a big stink. I guess people think of this cartoon dog as their own pet or something.

The last time they tried to cancel "Precious Poochie", four busloads of senior citizens from Leisure Towers showed up at the newspaper offices downtown and didn't leave until they got their way.

ACKNOWLEDGMENTS

Thanks to all the fans of the *Wimpy Kid* series for inspiring and motivating me to write these stories. Thanks to all of the booksellers across the nation for putting my books in kids' hands.

Thanks to my family for all the love and support. It's been fun to share this experience with you.

Thanks to the folks at Abrams for working hard to make sure this book happened. A special thanks to Charlie Kochman, my editor; Jason Wells, my publicist; and Scott Auerbach, managing editor extraordinaire.

Thanks to everyone in Hollywood for working so hard to bring Greg Heffley to life, especially Nina, Brad, Carla, Riley, Elizabeth, and Thor. And thanks, Sylvie and Keith, for your help and guidance.

ABOUT THE AUTHOR

Jeff Kinney is an online game developer and designer, and a #1 *New York Times* bestselling author. In 2009, Jeff was named one of *Time* magazine's 100 Most Influential People in the World. He spent his childhood in the Washington D.C.area and moved to New England in 1995. Jeff lives in southern Massachusetts with his wife and their two sons.

望子快乐

朱子庆

在一个人的一生中，"与有荣焉"的机会或有，但肯定不多。因为儿子译了一部畅销书，而老爸被邀涂鸦几句，像这样的与荣，我想，即使放眼天下，也没有几人领得吧。

儿子接活儿翻译《小屁孩日记》时，还在读着大三。这是安安他第一次领译书稿，多少有点紧张和兴奋吧，起初他每译几段，便飞鸽传书，不一会儿人也跟过来，在我面前"项庄舞剑"地问："有意思么？有意思么？"怎么当时我就没有作乐不可支状呢？于今想来，我竟很有些后悔。对于一个喂饱段子与小品的中国人，若说还有什么洋幽默能令我们"绝倒"，难！不过，当安安译成杀青之时，图文并茂，我得以从头到尾再读一遍，我得说，这部书岂止有意思呢，读了它使我有一种冲动，假如时间可以倒流，我很想尝试重新做一回父亲！我不免窃想，安安在译它的时候，不知会怎样腹诽我这个老爸呢！

我宁愿儿子是书里那个小屁孩！

你可能会说，你别是在做秀吧，小屁孩格雷将来能出息成个什么样子，实在还很难说……这个质疑，典型地出诸一个中国人之口，出之于为父母的中国人之口。望子成龙，一定要孩子出息成个什么样子，虽说初衷也是为了孩子，但最终却是苦了孩子。"生年不满百，常怀千岁忧。"现在，由于这深重的忧患，我们已经把成功学启示的模式都做到胎教了！而望子快乐，有谁想过？从小就快乐，快乐一生？惭愧，我也是看了《小屁孩日记》才想到这点，然而儿子已不再年少！我觉得很有些对不住儿子！

我从来没有对安安的"少年老成"感到过有什么不妥，毕竟少年老成使人放心。而今读其译作而被触动，此心才为之不安起来。我在想，比起美国的小屁孩格雷和他的同学们，我们中国的小屁孩们是不是活得不很小屁孩？是不是普遍地过于负重、乏乐和少年老成？而当他们将来长大，娶妻（嫁夫）生子（女），为人父母，会不会还要循此逻辑再造下一代？想想安安少年时，起早贪黑地读书、写作业，小四眼，十足一个书呆子，类似格雷那样的调皮、贪玩、小有恶搞、缰绳牢笼不住地敢于尝试和行动主义……太缺少了。印象中，安安最突出的一次，也就是读小学三年级时，做了一回带头大哥，拔了校园里所有自行车的气门芯并四处派发，仅此而已吧（此处请在家长指导下阅读）。

说点别的吧。中国作家写的儿童文学作品，很少能引发成年读者的阅读兴趣。安徒生童话之所以风靡天下，在于它征服了成年读者。在我看来，《小屁孩日记》也属于成人少年兼宜的读物，可以父子同修！谁没有年少轻狂？谁没有豆蔻年华？只不过呢，对于为父母者，阅读它，会使你由会心一笑而再笑，继以感慨系之，进而不免有所自省，对照和检讨一下自己和孩子的关系，以及在某些类似事情的处理上，自己是否欠妥？等等。它虽系成人所作，书中对孩子心性的把握，却准确传神；虽非心理学著作，对了解孩子的心理和行为，也不无参悟和启示。品学兼优和顽劣不学的孩子毕竟是少数，小屁孩格雷是"中间人物"的一个玲珑典型，着实招人怜爱——在格雷身上，有着我们彼此都难免有的各样小心思、小算计、小毛病，就好像阿Q，读来透着与我们有那么一种割不断的血缘关系，这，也许就是此书在美国乃至全球都特别畅销的原因吧！

最后我想申明的是，第一读者身份在我是弥足珍惜的，因为，宝贝儿子出生时，第一眼看见他的是医生，老爸都摊不上第一读者呢！

我眼中的 ......

好书，爱不释手！

★　读者　王汐子（女，2009年留学美国，攻读大学传媒专业）《小屁孩日记》在美国掀起的阅读风潮可不是盖的，在我留学美国的这一年中，不止一次目睹这套书对太平洋彼岸人民的巨大影响。高速公路上巨大的广告宣传牌就不用说了，我甚至在学校书店买课本时看到了这套书被大大咧咧地摆上书架，"小屁孩"的搞笑日记就这样理直气壮地充当起了美国大学生的课本教材！为什么这套书如此受欢迎？为什么一个普普通通的小男孩能让这么多成年人捧腹大笑？也许可以套用一个万能句式"每个人心中都有一个XXX"。每个人心中都有一个小屁孩，每个人小时候也有过这样的时光，每天都有点鸡毛蒜皮的小烦恼，像作业这么多怎么办啦，要考试了书都没有看怎么办啦……但是大部分时候还是因为调皮捣乱被妈妈教训……就这样迷迷糊糊地走过了"小屁孩"时光，等长大后和朋友们讨论后才恍然大悟，随即不禁感慨，原来那时候我们都一样呀……是呀，全世界的小屁孩都一样！

★　读者　zhizhimother（发表于2009-06-12）在杂志上看到这书的介绍，一时冲动在当当上下了单，没想到，一买回来一家人抢着看，笑得前仰后合。我跟女儿一人抢到一本，老公很不满意，他嘟囔着下一本出的时候他要第一个看。看多了面孔雷同的好孩子的书，看到这本，真是深有感触，我们的孩子其实都是这样长大的。

轻松阅读 捧腹大笑

★ 这是著名的畅销书作家小巫的儿子Sam口述的英语和中文读后感：I like *Diary* of a *Wimpy Kid* because Greg is an average child just like us. His words are really funny and the illustrations are hilarious. His stories are eventful and most of them involve silliness.

我喜欢《小屁孩日记》，因为Greg是跟我们一样的普通孩子。他的故事很好玩儿，令我捧腹大笑，他做的事情很搞笑，有点儿傻呼呼的。书里的插图也很幽默。

★ 读者 dearm暖baby（发表于2009-07-29）我12岁了，过生日时妈妈给我买了这样两本书，真的很有趣！一半是中文，一半是英文，彻底打破了"英文看不懂看下面中文"的局限！而且这本书彻底地给我来了次大放松，"重点中学"的压力也一扫而光！总之，两个字：超赞！

孩子爱上写日记了！

★ 读者 ddian2003（发表于2009-12-22）正是于丹的那几句话吸引我买下了这套书。自己倒没看，但女儿却用了三天学校的课余时间就看完了，随后她大受启发，连着几天都写了日记。

做个"不听话的好孩子"

★ 读者 水真爽（发表于2010-03-27）这套书是买给我上小学二年级的儿子的。有时候他因为到该读书的时间而被要求从网游下来很恼火。尽管带着气，甚至眼泪，可是读起这本书来，总是能被书中小屁孩的种种淘气出格行为和想法弄得哈哈大笑。这本书提醒了家长们好好留意观察这些"不怎么听话"的小屁孩们的内心世界，他们的健康成长需要成人的呵护引导，但千万不要把他们都变成只会"听大人话"的好孩子。

对照《小屁孩日记》分享育儿体验

★ 读者 gjrzj2002@＊＊＊.＊＊＊（发表于2010-05-21）看完四册书，我想着自己虽然不可能有三个孩子，但一个孩子的成长经历至今仍记忆犹新。儿子还是幼儿的时候，比较像曼尼，在爸妈眼中少有缺点，真是让人越看越爱，想要什么就基本上能得到什么。整个幼儿期父母对孩子肯定大过否定。上了小学，儿子的境地就不怎么从容了，上学的压力时时处处在影响着他，小家伙要承受各方面的压力，父母、老师、同学，太过我行我素、大而化之都是行不通的，比如没写作业的话，老师、家长的批评和提醒是少不了的，孩子在慢慢学着适应这种生活，烦恼也随之而来，这一阶段比较像格雷，虽然儿子的思维还没那么丰富，快乐和烦恼的花样都没那么多，但处境差不多，表扬和赞美不像以前那样轻易就能得到了。儿子青年时代会是什么样子我还不得而知，也不可想象，那种水到渠成的阶段要靠前面的积累，我希望自己到时候能平心静气，坦然接受，无论儿子成长成什么样子。

气味相投的好伙伴

★ 上海市外国语大学附属第一实验中学，中预10班，沈昕仪Elaine：《小屁孩日记》读来十分轻松。虽然没有用十分华丽的语言，却使我感受到了小屁孩那缤纷多彩的生活，给我带来无限的欢乐。那精彩的插图、幽默的文字实在是太有趣了，当中的故事在我们身边都有可能发生，让人身临其境。格雷总能说出我的心里话，他是和我有着共同语言的朋友。所以他们搞的恶作剧一直让我跃跃欲试，也想找一次机会尝试一下。不知别的读者怎么想，我觉得格雷挺喜欢出风头的。我也是这样的人，总怕别人无视了自己。当看到格雷蹦出那些稀奇古怪的点子的时候，我多想帮他一把啊——毕竟我们是"气味相投"的同类人嘛。另一方面，我身处在外语学校，时刻都需要积累英语单词，但这件事总是让我觉得枯燥乏味。而《小屁孩日记》帮了我的大忙：我在享受快乐阅读的同时，还可以对照中英文学到很多常用英语单词。我发现其实生活中还有很多事情值得我们去用笔写下来。即使是小事，这些童年的故事也是很值得我们回忆的。既然还生活在童年，还能够写下那些故事，又何乐而不为呢？

画出我心中的"小屁孩"

邓博笔下的赫夫利一家

读者@童_Cc.与@曲奇做的"小屁孩"手抄报

　　亲爱的读者，你看完这本书后，有什么感想吗？请来电话或是登录本书的博客与我们分享吧！等本书再版时，这里也许换上了你的读后感呢！

　　我们的电话号码是：020-83795744，博客地址是：blog.sina.com.cn/wimpykid，微博地址是：weibo.com/wimpywimpy。

悦读"小·屁孩"

《小·屁孩日记①——鬼屋创意》

在日记里，格雷记叙了他如何驾驭充满冒险
的中学生活，如何巧妙逃脱学校歌唱比赛，最重
要的是如何不让任何人发现他的秘密。他经常想
捉弄人反被人捉弄；他常常想做好事却弄巧成
拙；他屡屡身陷尴尬境遇竟逢"凶"化吉。他不
是好孩子，也不是坏孩子，就只是普通的孩子；
他有点自私，但重要关头也会挺身而出保护朋友……

《小·屁孩日记②——谁动了千年奶酪》

在《小·屁孩日记②》里，主人公格雷度过一个
没有任何奇迹发生的圣诞节。为打发漫长无聊的
下雪天，他和死党罗利雄心勃勃地想要堆出"世
界上最大的雪人"，却因为惹怒老爸，雪人被销
毁；格雷可是不甘寂寞的，没几天，他又找到乐
子了，在送幼儿园小朋友过街的时候，他制造了
一起"虫子事件"吓唬小朋友，并嫁祸罗利，从而
导致一场"严重"的友情危机……格雷能顺利化解
危机，重新赢得好朋友罗利的信任吗？

《小·屁孩日记③——好孩子不撒谎》

在本册里，格雷开始了他的暑假生活。慢
着，别以为他的假期会轻松愉快。其实他整个暑

假都被游泳训练班给毁了。他还自作聪明地导演了一出把同学齐拉格当成隐形人的闹剧，他以为神不知鬼不觉就可以每天偷吃姜饼，终于在圣诞前夜东窗事发，付出了巨大的代价……

《小·屁孩日记④——偷鸡不成蚀把米》

本集里，格雷仿佛落入了他哥哥罗德里克的魔掌中一般，怎么也逃脱不了厄运：他在老妈的威逼利诱下跟罗德里克学爵士鼓，却只能在一旁干看罗德里克自娱自乐；与好友罗利一起偷看罗德里克窝藏的鬼片，却不幸玩过火害罗利受伤，为此格雷不得不付出惨重代价——代替罗利在全

校晚会上表演魔术——而他的全部表演内容就是为一个一年级小朋友递魔术道具。更大的悲剧还在后面，他不惜花"重金"购买罗德里克的旧作业想要蒙混过关，却不幸买到一份不及格的作业。最后，他暑假误入女厕所的囧事还被罗德里克在全校大肆宣扬……格雷还有脸在学校混吗？他的日记还能继续下去吗？

《小·屁孩日记⑤——午餐零食大盗》

格雷在新的一年里展开了他的学校生活：克雷格老师的词典不翼而飞，于是每天课间休息时所有同学都被禁止外出，直至字典被找到；格雷的午餐零食从糖果变成了两个水果，他怀疑哥哥罗德里克偷了零食，誓要查出真相。因为午餐

零食闹的"糖荒"，让格雷精神不振，总是在下午的课堂上打瞌睡。格雷没有多余的零用钱，不能自己买糖果，于是他想到了自己埋下的

时光宝盒——里面放着三美元的钞票。格雷挖出时光宝盒，暂时缓解了"糖荒"。另一边厢，学校即将举行第一次的情人节舞会。格雷对漂亮的同班同学荷莉心仪已久，就决定趁舞会好好表现。在舞会上，他成功与荷莉互相交换了情人节卡片，并想邀请荷莉跳舞，于是他向人群中的荷莉走去……

《小·屁孩日记⑥——可怕的炮兵学校》

格雷想尽一切办法让老爸摆脱一些可怕的念头。格雷的老爸一直希望他能加强锻炼，就让他加入了周末的足球队。格雷在足球队吃尽了苦头：他先被教练派去当球童，在荆棘丛里捡球累了个半死；然后又被要求坐在寒风中观赛，冷得他直打哆嗦；后来他自以为聪明地选择了后备守门员的位置，最后却因为正选守门员受伤而不得不披挂上阵。在输掉足球比赛后，格雷觉得老爸因此而生气了。未想老爸又冒出另一个更可怕的念头：把格雷送进炮兵学校。格雷却自动请缨加入周末的童子军，因为这样一来他就不必再去参加足球训练了。然而，在童子军的父子营中，格雷又为老爸惹来麻烦……老爸决定在这个学期结束后，就立刻把格雷送进炮兵学校。眼看暑假就要开始了，格雷因此坐立不安……

《小·屁孩日记⑦——从天而降的巨债》

暑假刚开始，格雷就与老爸老妈展开了拉锯战：老爸老妈坚持认为孩子放暑假就应该到户外去活动，但格雷却宁愿躲在家里打游戏

机、看肥皂剧。不得已之下，格雷跟着死党罗利到乡村俱乐部玩，两人在那儿吃了一点东西，就欠下了83美元的"巨债"。于是，他们不得不想尽一切办法打工还债……

他们能把债务还清吗？格雷又惹出了什么笑话？

《小屁孩日记⑧——"头盖骨摇晃机"的幸存者》

老妈带全家上了旅行车，看到防晒霜和泳衣，格雷满心以为是去海滩度假，却原来只是去水上乐园——一个令格雷吃过很多苦头的地方，过去的不愉快记忆也就罢了，这次好不容易做好一切准备，广播却通知"因闪电天气停止营业"；回到家里又怎样呢？格雷发现他心爱的鱼  惨遭罗德里克宠物鱼的"毒口"；盼望已久的小狗阿甜来了，非但不是补偿，反而使格雷的生活一团糟；格雷发现救生员是希尔斯小姐，这使得他一改对于小镇游泳场的糟糕看法，小心眼儿活动起来；妈妈安排了一个格雷与爸爸改善关系的机会，可是格雷却用"甲壳虫小姐"召来了警察，搞得老爸灰溜溜的，他们关系更僵；老妈处心积虑安排格雷和死党罗利的一家去了海滩，格雷却又惹了祸……

我们可爱又倒霉的格雷啊，他该如何处理这一切？"头盖骨摇晃机"又是怎么回事？

《小·屁孩日记⑨——老妈不在家》

格雷的老妈在家庭会议中宣布自己要重返校园进修，这个消息让格雷父子措手不及：这意味着父子四人要自己做晚饭，还要分摊原来由老妈包揽的家务活……于是，他们开始了"灾民"般的生活。另一边厢，学校在新学期开了健康教育课，据说会讲一些老师从前避而不谈的内容；这门课煞有介事地要求家长签同意书，又让男生女生分班上课，这让格雷对课程的内容充满期待。

老妈不在家，格雷会在家里闹翻天吗？格雷在健康教育课上究竟能听到些什么内容？

《小·屁孩日记⑩——"屁股照片"风波》

小屁孩格雷在本集中，参加了学校组织的"关门"派对，在分组拍照游戏竞赛中，为了让其他组成员猜不出他们组拍的是谁而取得游戏的奖励，格雷和伙伴们想了各种办法，终于拍出了一幅大家都比较满意的照片，可是，老师认为他们的这幅照片拍的是人体某个部位，格调非常不雅……这让格雷和伙伴们觉得冤透了。事情最后落得什么样的结果呢？